HEAD OVER HEELS

Magee Sinclair keeps making costly blunders at her family's advertising agency, so when handsome Justin Kane, head of CycleMania, needs her to pose as his girlfriend for the weekend in exchange for a lucrative campaign, she has little choice but to say yes. Justin needs to cement a deal with Willoughby Bikes by impressing the Willoughbys while they bike trails together. But Magee has landed herself in major trouble — she doesn't know one end of a mountain bike from the other . . .

P R
P
Y
C
F
———
11
9v

3c
25

6 -

23

30

H E
I D
H G

———

CINDY PROCTER-KING

HEAD OVER HEELS

Complete and Unabridged

LINFORD
Leicester

First published in Great Britain in 2012

First Linford Edition
published 2014

A catalogue record for this book is available
from the British Library.

ISBN 978–1–4448–1865–9

Published by
F. A. Thorpe (Publishing)
Anstey, Leicestershire

Set by Words & Graphics Ltd.
Anstey, Leicestershire
Printed and bound in Great Britain by
T. J. International Ltd., Padstow, Cornwall

This book is printed on acid-free paper

Dedication

For Steve, who still sends me
head over heels

1

'*What?*' Justin Kane shot up from his desk, gripping the cordless phone so tight that his knuckles threatened to pop out of their skin. 'Tina, you can't do this to me.'

'Oh no? Well, I'm doing it, lover.' Justin's apparently soon-to-be ex-girlfriend's voice grated over the line. 'You've taken advantage of me for the last time.'

'Taken advantage?' Justin echoed like some slow-on-the-up-take parrot. She made him sound like a class-A jerk — as if she'd never had a hand in defining the casual nature of their relationship. He shook his head. 'I've never taken advantage of you any more than you've taken advantage of me.'

'Then let's say I've grown tired of the game.'

'Game? Tina, wait, this isn't a game.' Racking his brain for a recent list of sins he must have committed, Justin paced his efficiently organized office above the main Vancouver branch of his three CycleMania bike stores. He couldn't let Tina walk out on him now. The ink hadn't been applied to the deal with Willoughby Bikes yet.

He wanted that distributorship, and he needed Tina's help to get it.

'Besides,' he reminded her, 'I thought you liked what we have going together. I thought you liked it as much as I do.'

'I did like it, Justin, but things change. Or maybe I should say I've changed. Do you know what this weekend means to me?'

'Of course I do. The same as it does to me. The Willoughbys are flying in tomorrow, and we're taking them to Whistler.' The nearby mountain resort town would serve as the perfect backdrop for convincing Nathan Willoughby that CycleMania would fit seamlessly into the British bike manufacturer's growing worldwide 'family' of distributors. Justin had been counting on Tina's presence to cement the image of stability the English businessman demanded.

Tina snorted, rather delicately, but a snort all the same. 'Work is the first thing you would think of. But if you try real hard, you might come up with something else.'

Justin shoved a hand through his hair. He *had* been trying to decipher this disconcerting new dialect of Tina-speak, and he'd wound up several thousand syllables short. What did she expect? She'd propelled him into alien territory.

'It's your birthday?' he guessed.

'No, it's not my birthday. That was in April. It's July.' A huff of irritation resounded in his ear. 'Damn it, Justin, you're dense. You're either dense or you don't care.'

He frowned. When had his superficial and how-he-liked-her Tina transmuted into this perplexing pod person? Dragging in a breath, he focused on a

framed poster of the Cyclone —
Willoughby's pro-level, full-suspension
mountain bike — he'd hung on the wall
to inspire motivation.

'What then?' he asked.

'It's the six-month anniversary of our
first date.' Her tone assumed the
durability of quick-dry shellac.

Shit. He hadn't realized they were
keeping track. 'I didn't think that sort
of thing mattered to you.'

'I didn't, either — in *January*. Like I
said, I've changed. I'm thirty-four now,
Justin. Your mid-thirties might spell fun
and games to you, but my damn clock
is ticking. I want to get married, maybe
have a baby. I'm not prepared to wait
forever for you to decide you want the
same.'

'Come on, Tina, be reasonable. You
can't suddenly announce that you're
thinking babies and marriage when all
along we've agreed they're not on the
agenda.' Justin refused to repeat his
father's mistakes. He wouldn't mix
marriage and raising a family with

4

building a business, the way his father had done with his law practice. He'd thought Tina understood and accepted that about him.

'Oh please. I refuse to feel guilty for doing this. My needs have changed and yours haven't. It's that simple.'

'But to break up with me now? Nathan Willoughby and his wife expect to meet you. How can I take them to Whistler without you?'

'Tell them I have the flu.'

'And next week?'

'Tell them I fell off a cliff. I don't care. You'll think of something. You always do.' She paused. 'Listening to you, Justin, it's clear you don't want me. Not in the way I need. So why should I worry about this weekend? About whether or not you close this deal? Fend for yourself, big guy. That's what you've done all this time, anyway.' She hung up.

'Tina!' He punched in her number — and went straight to voice mail.

He tossed the cordless onto the desk.

Sitting, he scrubbed a hand over his face.

Hell, what a mess. What now? He couldn't go to Whistler without Tina. He'd look like a heel spending a carefree July weekend with the Willoughbys while Miss Personality Switcheroo supposedly lay in bed with a fever. Yet he couldn't say she'd dumped him, either. One indication that Justin's life was a shambles and Nathan Willoughby would write him off as unreliable. Justin could kiss the exclusive dealership rights for Willoughby Bikes in Vancouver and the distributorship for Western Canada goodbye.

He drummed his fingers on the desk. He might be an ignoramus when it came to the female of the species, but he knew his business and he wasn't willing to risk it. The four-month window he'd established for opening more bike stores depended on the financing the Willoughby Bikes deal would provide. Justin wasn't about to abandon that major step in his carefully constructed master life plan because Tina had sprouted maternal instincts the way most women sprouted leg hair.

Which left him with one option to pursue.

He needed a woman to replace Tina for the weekend.

And he had to find her fast.

★　★　★

Magee Sinclair glanced at her watch: 11:20. 'Time to suck up to the client,' she mumbled, tapping the papers for CycleMania's preliminary advertising plan on her desk. Usually, she didn't think of these touch-base lunches in frank terms. However, Justin Kane's account, with its phenomenal opportunity for growth, could singlehandedly pull Sinclair Advertising out of the red. Plus give her father necessary peace of mind. For that, Mr. Kane merited a bit of fawning over.

'He's not too bad to look at, either,' she murmured.

'Excuse me?' a condescending voice asked.

Jumping in her chair, Magee swiveled around. Her elbow bumped the CycleMania file folder. She grabbed, but before she could stop the folder's momentum, it skated across the desk, careened off her smartphone, and plopped into the wire mesh wastebasket.

Patti Slotnik, with her ever-ready smirk, leaned into the cubicle. 'What did you say, Maggie?'

Magee clutched the papers. *Why must the woman continually mangle my name?*

And sneak up on her? She was lucky she hadn't lost her grip on the hard copy Justin Kane had requested.

'Nothing. Thinking out loud.' She tried to sound breezy and unconcerned. 'The name's Magee, as you know. Short A, hard G. Like the surname. My mother's birth name.' *So get it right.* 'If it's too hard to remember, I could write it phonetically.' She pasted on a sweet smile.

'Ah,' Patti replied. 'My bad.' Her mud-brown eyebrows rose. 'Sure you don't need help? I thought you'd left for your meeting already. I was about to drop you a note. I'm happy to lend a hand if you're feeling stressed.'

'No, thank you. I know you're more than willing to help, but I have everything under control.' Magee possessed enough of Patti's let-me-ease-your-burden messages to wallpaper the ad agency's break room. She certainly didn't require another.

'Just offering,' Patti sing-songed before moving on.

That's it. Be gone. Good riddance. Magee realized her fellow account executive didn't respect her, and, in some ways, she couldn't blame Patti. Magee hadn't worked for the ad agency as long as Patti had. Yet, as the owner's daughter, Magee stood to inherit the account director position her father planned to create, effectively making her Patti's boss. The woman's resentment was only natural, although irritating up the wazoo. And the mix-up with the billboards in January — an event of mega-embarrassing proportions that had fallen on Magee's shoulders — had supplied Patti with additional reason to smirk.

At this rate, Magee would have the respect of a flea by the time she assumed the new post. *If* she assumed it. At the moment, she didn't feel too deserving. In her current role as one of four AEs, her responsibilities included overseeing the campaigns Creative Services produced for her clients. If she'd done her job properly the last several months, her father's advertising agency wouldn't be out three major accounts. And she wouldn't feel trapped in an endless game of Pick Up Sticks.

She placed the papers on her desk and bent to retrieve the folder from the trash. Her fingers jammed on a snag in the mesh. A nail caught and ripped. *Ouch.*

Squeezing shut her eyes, she lifted her hand.

Be okay. Please be okay.

She peeked at her hand, and her stomach dropped. *Oh my God.* She'd ruined her beautiful spa manicure! The expensive exfoliating scrub and paraffin dip mani-pedi she'd indulged in this morning to wow Mr. Hottie Pants Kane. A huge crescent of missing raspberry polish mocked her from the ragged nail of her middle finger.

Not her pinky. Not her thumb. Not any finger that might escape notice.

But her freaking screw-you-buddy finger.

Magee, how could you? When would she stop messing up? Hadn't her parents hammered into her that client meetings required a professional image? For a future account director — the agency's first ever account director — that included a skirt, heels, and ten flawless, skillfully polished nails.

Not nine perfect nails and one screw-you torn to the quick. *Ten.*

She collated the papers and returned them to the folder, then stuffed the preliminary plan and her tablet into her briefcase. From a desk drawer, she grabbed nail clippers, her best crystal file, and the bottle of raspberry polish she'd bought on a whim before leaving the spa. Hey, maybe she *was* learning, after all.

She hurried to the ladies room for repairs.

★ ★ ★

'More ice water, miss?'

'Please.' As the waiter refilled her goblet, Magee stared at her plate and sighed. Whatever had possessed her to order an enormous Caesar salad laced with enough garlic to do in a mob boss? And the anchovies . . . She hated the salty devils. Detested them. Why, then, had those words of doom, 'Heavy on the anchovies,' escaped her mouth?

As if you don't know the answer, Magee.

Justin Kane. He of the lustrous coal-black hair and piercing slate-blue eyes, which, at the moment, remained fixed on the hard copy of her preliminary advertising plan. The man confused her something fierce.

She picked up her fork. Even with the bread basket and bottle of balsamic vinegar separating them across the restaurant table, Justin Kane made her nervous. He always had, from the instant they'd met four months ago in her ultimately successful bid to woo the CycleMania account from a rival agency. However, today Justin's troubling effect on her had mushroomed. Despite the unexpected adjustments to her manicure, she'd arrived at the restaurant her standard fifteen minutes early to discover him already seated, a predatory glint in his eyes.

Almost as if . . . as if he *knew* her little secret behind snaring his account and was biding his time before ambushing her.

But he couldn't know. How would he

have found out? It had just been one teensy, tiny white lie.

Not a stark white, either. More of a subtle cream.

Strangely, the distinction didn't comfort her. If anything, she felt worse.

She jabbed her fork at a gargantuan crouton. Instead of piercing the tidbit, the tines bounced it off her plate. Glancing sidelong at Justin, she crept a hand toward the crouton. He looked up. She pinky-kicked the crouton beneath the cloth napkin and flashed an overeager smile.

Fortunately, he didn't notice the crouton's acrobatics. His gaze lowered to her salad.

'You're not eating. Is something wrong with the Caesar?' He smoothed the triple-striped tie he wore with a conservative gray tweed blazer.

'Oh no,' she answered too brightly. 'I had a huge breakfast. I should have ordered the half-size salad.'

His eyes narrowed, and the predatory glint she'd noticed upon her arrival returned. He glanced at the preliminary plan, then back up. He rubbed a thumb along his strong, square jaw.

Magee's heart thundered against her ribs. *This is it. The jig's up.*

She waited for the guillotine blade to drop.

He opened his mouth. She sucked in a breath.

His mouth snapped shut. Her breath whooshed out.

'What?' Her voice squeaked. If the guillotine didn't get her, the suspense surely would.

'You've done your homework. I like that.'

Her homework? *Phew.* He didn't know her secret, after all.

Good on ya, girl. Stay cool.

Placing aside the hard copy, Justin retrieved her tablet from the empty third place setting and browsed through the presentation again. 'Your idea to use magazines like *Mountain Bike Frenzy* sounds expensive, but worth it. I'm impressed.'

Magee tucked a lock of hair behind one ear. Leaning forward, she bracketed her hands — with their ten flawless *short* raspberry nails — around her salad plate. The fishy scent of anchovies assailed her nostrils, but she ignored it.

'I'm glad to hear you say that, Justin, because the market research clearly indicates two distinct audiences for CycleMania's advertising purposes. The first is the recreational cyclist your stores currently target through local Internet, radio, and newspaper spots. That approach is working well. Aside from updating the ads, I see no reason to change it. Streamlining the website and increasing the company's social networking efforts will make a difference, too.' Her finger bumped the crouton out from beneath the napkin, exposing it to Justin's line of vision. Discreetly, she curled her pinky around the crouton and nudged it toward the table edge. Another nudge . . .

Tik-plop.

The crouton ricocheted off her chair

arm, landing on her lap.

'The second target audience,' she continued with as much professionalism as she could muster, given the crouton on her skirt, 'is the cycling enthusiast. Specifically, the hard-core mountain biker. Young. Hip. Radical. Intense. Serious about the sport and willing to pay top dollar for the latest innovations. For this particular audience, we need a medium with a concentrated focus. *Mountain Bike Frenzy* is an excellent example.'

Justin nodded, and she released a breath. She'd sold him. She could sense it.

'This is where Willoughby Bikes comes in,' he said, returning her tablet to the table. He dipped his spoon into his minestrone.

'Exactly.' Taking her cue from her client, Magee dug into her salad. She really did love garlic. Too bad her breath preferred mints. 'With the manufacturer picking up half the cost to have their bikes featured in your ads, it's a win-win. Plus, the similarity between store and product names lends to great short copy ideas. Picture a glossy spread in *Mountain Bike Frenzy* ending with something snappy like, 'The Cyclone. Available exclusively at CycleMania.' It has a nice ring to it, wouldn't you agree?'

'Provided I sign the deal with Nathan Willoughby.'

'You will.'

'Yeah? I don't know anymore.'

Magee's scalp tingled. She'd never before heard Justin Kane speak of the CycleMania — Willoughby Bikes deal with less than absolute confidence. 'Why do you say that?'

He didn't answer, just eyed her, his ring-less ring finger tapping staccato time on the table.

She moistened her lips. 'Uh, Justin?'

'Something's happened.'

'What?' *Please don't say this 'something' could affect the deal.*

'It's personal, but . . . it could affect the deal.'

Argh. Magee held her breath. The substantial advertising revenue inherent in Justin's deal with Willoughby Bikes would help repair the financial damage she'd caused her father's advertising agency these last several months. If Justin lost the deal, his expansion plans for the CycleMania chain of bike stores — an additional source of revenue for the agency — would be postponed. He'd said so during one of their many conversations leading to the development of the preliminary advertising plan. He needed the deal with Willoughby Bikes to make his expansion fly, and she needed him to get it.

'Something personal?' She shook her head. 'I don't understand.'

His gaze drifted over her. Abruptly, his finger stopped tapping. 'You will. You see, I need your help.'

'Not an issue,' she said without missing a beat. 'What can I do?'

'Come with me to Whistler.'

Her pulse fluttered. 'What?' She put down her romaine-laden fork.

Justin regarded her with his deep-set, thickly lashed eyes. 'Nathan Willoughby wants to spend a few days in Whistler and Vancouver checking out my stores and the mountain biking trails in the area before we sign the deal. Right now he's in California with his wife, doing the same with the new U.S. distributor. He arrives in Vancouver tomorrow.'

'With his wife?'

'Kathryn. Yes.'

Oookay. Magee rubbed her neck. She must be suffering from an anchovy-induced stupor, because she still couldn't make the connection. 'And you need me . . . why?'

'It's a couples thing. You know, relaxation before business. At any rate, Tina, my girlfriend — ' Justin practically ground out the word ' — let me know an hour ago that she's not coming.'

'Oh.' Magee gazed at him. 'Is she sick?'

'No. She dumped me.'

'D-dumped you?' In Magee's world,

that meant he didn't *have* a girlfriend.

'Yes,' he said without cracking a smile. 'And that presents me with a problem. I can't go to Whistler alone. I need you to come with me, as a replacement, of sorts, for Tina.'

Magee blinked instead of insulting her client by bursting out laughing. The man's girlfriend had cut him loose *an hour ago* and he was already cruising for a replacement to accommodate a deal?

Her opinion of Justin Kane slipped several notches.

'It's business, you understand,' he continued. 'Willoughby Bikes is grounded in the long-standing English traditions of loyalty, family honor, and trust. Stability in business and relationships is important to both Nathan Willoughby and his father. That's why the company invested so many years building a reputation overseas before entering the North American market. That's also why I can't tell Nathan that Tina turfed me.'

'Because then he wouldn't find you desirable?' Magee asked before she could stop herself.

'In a way. If my personal life isn't under control, how can Nathan believe that my business is?'

A male perspective, if she'd ever heard one. And she'd heard enough in her twenty-nine years to last her ninety, thank you very much.

She swigged her ice water. 'So what you're saying is that by telling him you could risk the deal.'

'Precisely.' He had the audacity to smile. 'I'm glad you understand.' He finished his minestrone.

'To be honest, I don't.' She swept the crouton off her lap and ground it into the floor with her shoe. Other than for the stated business complications, didn't Justin care that his girlfriend had broken up with him? If so, he hid it well. 'I don't understand why you need me. Can't you ask a female friend?'

'You seem upset. Why?'

'Because. I don't like the sound of this.'

'You don't have to like it. You just have to help me.'

'Again, why me?'

He stared at her. 'I can't take any woman along. I need someone who mountain bikes.'

Magee's stomach flip-flopped. She couldn't mountain bike to save her life. Thinking about the sport terrified her.

There it was, her secret exposed . . . if she chose to expose it.

But she couldn't tell Justin the truth *now*. If she did, he might terminate his contract with her father's advertising agency — and she wouldn't blame him.

She'd screwed up.

Again.

She had no choice but to go along with whatever her client suggested.

'I see.' Her homemade noose tightened. 'That makes sense.'

★ ★ ★

Justin straightened in his chair. For a second, he'd thought Magee would turn him down, and then where would he be? During his six months with Tina, he hadn't looked at another woman. All right, he'd looked, but he hadn't touched. He might not believe in marriage before forty, but that didn't mean he'd lost faith in monogamy, particularly in this age of STDs and crazy women blathering their personal lives all over the Internet.

'Then you'll do it?' he asked Magee.

She nodded as if he'd sentenced her to face a firing squad.

Odd. He'd offered her a chance to go wheel-skiing at Whistler, one of the few local mountain biking venues she hadn't tried. Or so she'd said when he'd signed with her advertising agency two months ago. He'd thought she'd feel ecstatic. Instead, her creamy complexion had assumed an ashy tinge.

'Remember,' he told her for added incentive, 'what's good for CycleMania is good for Sinclair Advertising. We both stand to gain financially from this deal.'

Her light green gaze darted away. 'I'm game. What do you want me to do?' She ran her fingers through the chin-length blond hair framing her face. The color reminded him of liquid honey, natural and appealing.

'Accompany me to Whistler for the weekend as my girlfriend. A long weekend, to be specific. The Willoughbys arrive tomorrow — Thursday. We'll meet them at the airport and leave for the mountain right away. We won't return to Vancouver until Sunday. Will that work for you?'

She looked him square in the eyes. 'I'll make it work, Justin. You're a valuable client. I wouldn't want you to lose this deal.'

'Good, we're on the same wavelength.' The cell phone in his pants pocket vibrated, signaling an incoming text. He rat-a-tapped his hands on the table. He'd scheduled a tour of warehouse sites with a realtor for this afternoon. The woman liked to check in. He should leave and let her know he was on his way.

'You don't have to bring your mountain bike,' he advised Magee. 'We'll use rentals from the CycleMania store in Whistler. As for what to pack, we'll go out for dinner once or twice. Also, bring your hiking boots and a bathing suit for the hot tub.'

'Hot tub?'

'At my parents' cabin. They have a place in a subdivision near Whistler. Three bedrooms, so there's plenty of space. Except, of course, we'll have to share.'

'We?' She winced. 'As in you and me?'

'Well, I don't think Nathan would appreciate it if I tried to bunk with his wife.' Justin tucked the printout of the preliminary plan into his briefcase. When he glanced up, the ashen cast to Magee's skin had intensified. 'Don't worry, this isn't a convoluted attempt at sexual harassment. We'll pretend to share a room. I'll sleep in another.'

'But . . . we're supposed to be . . . lovers?'

Clearly, the prospect of participating in the charade disturbed her. However, he didn't have time to address her concerns now. He'd have to do so later. 'That's the idea. I need to keep this simple, Magee. Believe it or not, I don't usually engage in deception to get what I want. In order to pull off this weekend, I need to think of you as Tina. In other words, as my lover.'

'How? We barely know each other.'

'I have a plan to correct that.'

Her pert nose crinkled. 'What?'

'Practice, Miss Sinclair. Lots of it.'

2

'He wants you to pretend to be his lover?' Susannah Deshane's bubbling laughter bounced off the bedroom walls in Magee's small apartment. 'Magee, how do you keep finding yourself in these nutty situations?'

'A mess,' Magee clarified for her neighbor and friend. 'It's not a situation, it's a mess. A major one.' Tightening the sash of her satin bathrobe, she scoured her cramped walk-in closet for an appropriate outfit for the practice date Justin had proposed before he'd bolted out of their lunch to meet his realtor.

A shrewd one, that Justin Kane. A practice date might settle her nerves — or at least help her prepare for tomorrow.

When the Willoughbys arrived.

Gulp.

She glanced over her shoulder. 'I have no one to blame for this current mess but myself,' she said to Susannah. 'I never should have lied to Justin about the mountain biking in the first place.'

'You can blame me.' Susannah joined Magee in the tiny closet. 'It was my brainwave that you tell him you're an expert mountain biker. You wanted to win his account so badly.' Susannah flipped through the clothes on the opposite rod.

'Just because you suggested the idea didn't mean I had to do it.' That decision had been hers alone, the last in a string of questionable choices. Considering she'd realized Justin would only switch advertising agencies to secure the insight of an account executive who mountain biked, her fib had been a shady method to land his business. 'At least Dad's still on holidays. I couldn't face telling him right now that I've made another mistake.'

'Will you tell him when he returns?'

'I haven't decided. It took forever to convince him to take Mom on this vacation. I don't want him to regret going.' Also, she wanted a chance to rectify the situation before it became necessary to tell him.

She studied a short knit dress. *Too clingy*.

'I want him to have faith in me again, Susannah,' she added, riffling through her clothes. 'If I'm going to accept this promotion to account director, I need to feel like I've earned it. Yet every time I turn around, I lose the agency money . . . or clients . . . or both! No matter how hard I try, I screw up. First the billboards, then the Barnacle Beer ad. And let's not forget the little day-to-day snafus. I swear I'll pull my hair out if I can't get my act together soon.'

Susannah's muffled giggle drifted to Magee's ears. Spinning in the closet, she squinted at the rear view of her friend. Susannah searched the opposite rod, her long blond curls bobbling around her shaking shoulders.

'What?' Magee asked.

'The billboard mix-up.' Susannah faced her. 'You have to admit, that one was funny.'

'Susannah!' Magee smacked her friend's arm. ' 'Do Your Buns Get Freezer Burn?' is *not* appropriate copy for sun block. And 'To Soothe And Protect' only marginally suits freezer bags.'

'Yeah, but the buns line looked fantastic splashed on the billboard of the handsome cop slathering sunscreen on the female model. Come on, Magee, you thought it was cute, too.'

Magee drew in a breath. 'It was mildly entertaining. But my father wasn't impressed with the mix-up, and neither were the Sear-Soothe people — and *I* can't figure out how it happened. Nope. No more, Susannah. I lost two clients over that disaster. I don't intend to lose another.' Squaring her shoulders, she selected a knee-length black skirt for her friend's inspection. 'How's this?'

Susannah stuck a finger down her throat. 'Gag. This is a date, old buddy, old pal. Remember, he's your *lover*.'

How could she forget that most intriguing detail? Justin Kane might treat his women like dirt — otherwise, why would Tina Whoever dump him? — but his eyes, body, and deep, sensual voice inspired fantasies of Magee locking him in her bedroom, oh, for the next fifty years.

She waved a hand at the row of clothes. 'You choose.'

Susannah grinned. 'With pleasure.'

'Great. I'm hot.' And bothered. Extremely so when she thought of Justin Kane. 'I need a pop. Want one?'

'No, thanks.'

Leaving her friend in the closet, Magee strode barefoot to the miniscule kitchen of her U-shaped apartment. She grabbed a diet cola from the fridge. She'd worked for her father for over three years. She could afford to rent a newer place if she wanted. However, she loved the flavor of her Kitsilano neighborhood with its tree-lined side-walks and old houses remodeled into apartments. The layout of her suite left something to be desired, with the bathroom accessible only through the living room, but Magee didn't mind sacrificing convenience for the nobler pursuit of character. If doing so entailed traipsing through the kitchen and living room to reach the bathroom in the dead of night, that was fine by her.

She set the pop can on the counter and tinkled ice cubes into a glass. A huge gray cat meowed at her through the gable window spanning the length of the kitchen in the top-floor apart-ment.

Magee pushed open the window. The cat sauntered in, front paws meeting the counter with a grace that belied his bulk.

'Hi, Monster. Time for your milk, baby?' Magee picked up the cat and stroked his soft fur. Monster tolerated her cuddling for thirty seconds before scrambling to the floor. Magee filled a saucer with the evaporated milk she stored in the fridge for the cat. Purring, Monster slurped his treat. Flying flecks of heavy milk dotted the linoleum.

'Magee?' Susannah appeared in the bedroom doorway, several garments slung over her arm. 'You're feeding that cat again?'

'As if you don't when he visits you. I can't let him starve.'

A wry smile tipped Susannah's mouth. 'His real owners feed him daily. In case you hadn't noticed, it's 7:35. Aren't your dinner reservations with Justin for eight?'

Magee zapped a glance to the wall clock. 'Omigod, you're right. He'll be here in ten minutes.' She sloshed the diet cola into the glass, then scurried to the bedroom. 'What are my choices?' Sitting on the bed, she sipped the cold pop.

'Well, you said he's taking you to The Dock. That's outdoors, but it's a warm night. Perfect for something short and sexy.'

34

'I'm not trying to seduce him, Susannah.'

'Why not? He's your lover.'

Magee rolled her eyes.

Susannah held out a vintage, fuchsia leather mini-dress. 'How about this?' she asked.

'Not on your life. That's my hooker outfit from last Halloween.'

'It's cute.'

Magee jabbed an imaginary buzzer on the bed. '*Bzzzt*. Try again.'

Monster, evidently finished his milk, strutted in from the kitchen, hopped on the mattress, and resumed purring. Gripping the cool glass of cola in one hand, Magee petted the cat as Susannah presented another dress.

'This?'

Magee shook her head. 'Too short.'

'This?'

'Too flirty.'

'*This?*'

Magee's heart pounded. 'Too tight!'

Susannah planted a hand on her shorts-clad hip. 'Magee, other than your work clothes, every summer outfit you own is either too short, too flirty, or too tight.'

'Not the black skirt.'

'You are *not* wearing the black skirt. Time is of the essence here. Take a leap of faith and close your eyes.'

Magee obeyed.

Rustle, rustle.

'You can open them again.'

Magee opened her eyes.

Susannah stood beside the bed, shaking out a beautiful turquoise slip dress.

'Susannah, yes! I forgot about that dress.' Magee glided a finger over the cool silk. She bit her lip. 'Uh, maybe not. Look at the skinny straps. I don't own a bra in a coordinating color anymore.'

Susannah shrugged. 'Go braless. It wouldn't be the first time. You're lucky in that department.'

In other words, Magee's barely-Bs didn't strictly require a bra.

'But to not wear one *this* time?'

'Honey, you're not thinking clearly. Repeat after me, 'Justin Kane is my lover.''

'Justin Kane is . . . my lover.' A delicious thrill vibrated through Magee as she spoke the words that would guide her thoughts and actions over the next three days. Her body warmed in strategic places. Even her cheeks heated to a burn.

She placed her cola glass on the nightstand, accepted the dress from Susannah, and began to change. She was running out of options.

Susannah strolled to the dresser and withdrew a wispy silk wrap in shades of turquoise and deep pink. The bright tulip shade almost matched Magee's modified raspberry manicure. Clever friend.

'Cover up with this if you're shy.'

'Thanks. You're a genius.' Magee arranged the wrap around her shoulders, then stepped into flat silver sandals. Standing at the dresser mirror, she finger-fluffed her hair around her

37

face and slipped dangly silver earrings into her lobes.

Susannah applauded. 'Now the finishing touch. Perfume.'

Magee grabbed the nearest bottle. She read the label. '*Possessed*. Perfect. That's how I feel after agreeing to this weekend.' Aiming at the base of her throat, she pressed the sprayer.

T-sss.

She lifted her finger, but the pump stayed down.

Ssssssst! T-ssssst!

'Ack! It's jammed!'

A dense cloud of sultry perfume engulfed her.

She yanked the sticky sprayer top. The round bottle slipped out of her hands and bounced on the carpet, spitting perfume on her legs before the pump finally dislodged.

It was not her day!

'Magee!' Coughing, Susannah tented her hands over her nose.

Magee kicked the bottle toward her friend. 'Trash that for me, will you? And make sure Monster's okay. I have to clean up!' Racing through the kitchen, she cursed the dimwit who'd situated the bathroom on the other side of the U.

At the bathroom sink, she dampened a washcloth and dabbed it gingerly to her upper chest. On top of everything else, it would not do to wet her dress.

At the third dab, a knock rapped on the apartment door.

Her heart flew into her throat. *Justin!*

No time. She had no more time. Had she de-Possessed herself sufficiently? Justin Kane didn't strike her as a man who liked to be kept waiting.

Shaking her shoulders loose, she opened the bathroom door.

Play it cool, like nothing's wrong.

And pray he's lost his sense of smell.

★ ★ ★

Justin planned to kiss her and get it over with.

Not as soon as she answered the

door, though. That seemed crass. However, in order to pull off their roles as lovers, they'd need to kiss in front of the Willoughbys at some point over the weekend. They might as well accomplish the deed before dinner and abolish any awkwardness Magee might be feeling right from the beginning.

He raised his hand to knock again. Before his knuckles met the wood, the door swung inward and a blast of heavy perfume seared his nostrils.

His eyes watered. *Possessed.* He'd recognize the cloying scent anywhere. It had been Tina's favorite perfume, and she'd never missed the opportunity to announce the expensive brand to anyone who'd asked.

At least Tina had applied the musky scent with a light touch. Magee emitted enough vapors to asphyxiate a troop of enemy soldiers.

'Hi,' she said in a chipper voice. 'I have to grab my purse. Come in.'

She didn't mention the perfume. Didn't she realize she'd overdosed?

Nose twitching, Justin trailed her into the apartment. Only the distraction of her bare, tanned legs stretching off into forever beneath her sassy, short dress prevented him from asking for a gas mask.

She left him standing in the living room, and the perfume stench slowly dissipated. Rocking on his heels with his hands in his trouser pockets, Justin surveyed her apartment. When Magee had provided her Kitsilano address, he'd assumed she rented an apartment. However, he'd expected something new and contemporary from the heiress-apparent to Sinclair Advertising. This house, while solid-looking from the street, appeared every day of its eightyish years. Magee had decorated the place nicely. Rattan furniture cheered the living room and potted plants flanked a bookshelf. In contrast, an ancient radiator rested against the wall and, in the entrance, a white-painted ladder climbed into a drafty attic opening.

What did she see in the place? Without a doubt, she could afford better.

Justin's lips curled. He sounded like his father — the last thing he wanted. And this whole fake-girlfriend scheme could have been torn from the pages of the Richard Kane how-to handbook.

But Justin was stuck. Only a fool would change his plans now that Magee had agreed to help him.

After another moment, his partner-in-mischief sailed into the living room, a tiny silver evening bag hanging from her shoulder. A tall blonde carrying a hairy gray cat accompanied her. Neither woman appeared to notice the sickly-sweet perfume billowing around Magee.

'This is my friend, Susannah.' Magee introduced the woman to Justin. 'She lives in the other upstairs apartment. Susannah, this is Justin Kane.'

'Hi,' Susannah said. The overgrown cat bared its vampire fangs and hissed at Justin. Susannah grabbed the cat's paw as it swiped toward him.

'Whoa!' He stepped back. He wasn't partial to cats, but neither did he dislike them. What did this one have against him?

'Monster!' Magee admonished the animal. She wagged her finger in the feline's whiskered face. 'Bad cat,' she said in a curiously soothing tone. 'You hear me? Baaad.'

The aptly named Monster squirmed in Susannah's arms and released a sour meow.

'Okay, okay.' Susannah lowered the cat to the carpet. Ears flattening, the beast dashed into the kitchen, around the stove, and out of sight.

Magee groaned. 'He's hiding under the bed again, I just know it.' Long-lashed eyes widening, she glanced at Justin. 'Sorry. I shouldn't have let him in. He's shy with strangers.'

'Unless they come bearing food,' her friend said.

Magee chuckled. Fiddling with her purse strap, she asked Susannah, 'Can

43

you find him and put him out after Justin and I go? I shouldn't leave him inside all night without a litter box.'

Susannah nodded. 'No problem.'

The soles of Justin's feet tingled. 'You don't have a litter box?' He lifted one shoe and wiggled the heel.

'I don't need a box for Monster. That's the Campbells' department.' Quickly, she added, 'The couple in the basement suite. Monster's theirs, not mine. I just feed him from time to time.'

Justin turned up a hand. 'Why?'

Magee's gaze swung to Susannah's in a time-honored female expression Justin loosely interpreted as *Men*.

'In case he's hungry,' Magee replied as if the answer were obvious.

'He's a co-op cat,' Susannah chimed in. 'The Campbells work twelve-hour shifts in a hospital, so Magee started feeding the cat while they're gone. Next thing we knew, the rest of us were feeding him, too. All four apartments.'

Now Justin had heard everything. 'A co-op cat that's afraid of people?'

'Shy,' Magee corrected. 'He's *shy* around *strangers*. There's a difference.'

'Uh huh.' And that difference was that apparently the cat was as crazy as Magee Sinclair.

Funny how Justin hadn't noticed this quirky side to her before.

But then, until nine hours ago, he'd been devoted to Tina.

As devoted as he could manage at this stage of his life, anyway.

Before tonight, he'd never allowed himself to think of Magee as anything other than a business associate. However, now, *because* of business, he had to take a personal interest in her.

To think in terms of touching her, kissing her.

Right, he still needed to kiss her.

Preferably without Susannah watching.

'Ready to go?' he asked, stepping in to help Magee adjust a frothy shawl thing around her shoulders. He maintained a polite distance, avoiding a lungful of Possessed.

She nodded, thanking him, then said goodnight to her friend. 'Don't forget Monster.'

'I won't,' Susannah said. 'Have fun.'

Justin placed his hand on Magee's upper back. As he escorted her to the door, his fingers skimmed smooth, warm flesh beside a spaghetti-thin dress strap. Her skin pebbled beneath his touch, creating a ticklish hum against his palm.

He lowered his head to her ear. 'Is it wise to leave someone in your apartment?' he half-whispered.

'Susannah has a key,' Magee announced, whirling to her friend. 'You'll lock up for me, won't you, neighbor?'

'Consider it done. And if you promise to tell me all about your date, I won't even steal anything.' Susannah winked.

'See?' Magee shrugged. 'She's trustworthy.'

'Point taken,' Justin conceded. Obviously, the two women were close. Magee was nothing like Tina, who would no more allow a neighbor to stay alone in her apartment than she would a colony of red ants.

But then maybe he didn't know Tina as well as he'd thought. He'd never pegged her for mother material, that was for certain. Until this morning, she hadn't provided indication that she *liked* kids. Was he so consumed by work that he hadn't heeded her signals?

He set his jaw. Any soul-searching needed to wait until after he signed the Willoughby Bikes deal.

One step at a time. That was his motto, and he was sticking to it.

He and Magee exited the apartment. The door clicked shut on Susannah, leaving them alone on the diminutive landing between the two upstairs apartments. The strong scent of Magee's perfume swept around them like a thick coastal mist.

Justin steeled himself against the impending onslaught. *Carpe diem. Seal off the nasal passages and seize the day.* Or, in this case, the woman.

Clasping her hand, he tugged her close. 'How about we start practicing right away?'

She blinked. 'What do you mean?'

'A kiss.'

'A kiss?'

'A kiss.' The idea increased in appeal every time he said it. He hovered his mouth above hers. Her pink lips parted.

God, she was beautiful.

He inhaled. A mistake. Possessed coursed up his nose and blazed a trail down his throat.

He leaned back. Regrouped. Tried again. This time closing his stinging eyes.

An image of Tina's angry face swam into his mind.

Damn it. He couldn't kiss Magee under these conditions. No way. No how. No chance.

He needed air — and a guilt-free conscience.

Susannah's movements within the apartment foyer provided the ideal cop-out: would she interrupt them?

Magee must have shared his concern, because they glanced at the door in tandem.

'On second thought, let's save the kiss for later,' Justin said. He held his breath while she nodded.

She descended the staircase ahead of him, out of earshot.

'Much later,' he mumbled. Like after she'd taken a shower.

* * *

Magee rubbed the stem of her wineglass and slipped a wobbly smile to the middle-aged couple sending her strange looks from the table nearest hers and Justin's. As their practice date progressed, it grew more and more apparent that she wasn't fooling anyone. Not one stinking soul.

Not the lanky guy in valet parking who'd sneezed several times while helping her out of Justin's sleek, black sports car.

Not the headwaiter who'd seated

them as far from the other diners as possible, on the portion of the terrace restaurant bordering Beach Avenue.

Not the tittering party of four sitting downwind from them in the warm, mid-July ocean breeze fluttering off English Bay.

And definitely not Justin.

Magee had to face the facts. She reeked. She knew it, and so did every other patron within a three-table radius at The Dock.

Despite her attempts to banish the Possessed from her body — at home and then again in the restaurant washroom upon their arrival — the heavy perfume lingered. It was like the musky fragrance had saturated her every pore and now discharged at regular intervals like a time-released migraine capsule.

At least Justin had spared her the embarrassment of telling her she smelled. However, she'd noticed him brushing his nose as they'd walked into the restaurant. And, in the car on the drive over, only a deaf person would have missed the pinched-nostril tone to his voice indicating he'd breathed through his mouth. He hadn't been as crafty as he'd probably thought when he'd changed his mind about their practice kiss outside her apartment door, either.

No, she knew the truth. He would have suffocated had he kissed her. He might have collapsed on the spot!

She had to muster serious damage control if she wanted to maintain Justin's faith in her ability to handle the weekend. She needed resolve. Steely-eyed determination. *Fake it until you make it*.

Therein lay the secret to her success.

Halfway through their meals of grilled Pacific salmon, she set down her fork and raised her wineglass in a toast. 'Here's to this weekend, Justin. To Willoughby Bikes and CycleMania. I promise I'll do whatever I can to ensure the path to signing the deal runs smoothly.'

Justin smiled. Lifting his glass, he responded, 'To our little charade . . . '

'To us . . . '

'To you — my newfound Tina. I can't thank you enough, Magee. I'd be up to my ass in concrete if you hadn't agreed to help me.'

Magee maintained her composed facade. It wasn't like she'd had much choice. As he'd pointed out at lunch, her father's company would also benefit from the deal.

And, oh boy, did Sinclair Advertising need the revenue.

Justin sipped his pinot gris. 'Speaking of the charade, I'm worried about confusing names in front of Nathan. I should start calling you Tina tonight.'

Magee's wineglass knocked her teeth. 'You want to call me Tina?' Had she missed something?

Nodding, he divided his remaining salmon into serviceable mouthfuls. 'You'll have to use her name when we're with the Willoughbys,' he said as he swabbed a forkful in dill sauce. 'It

can't hurt to get used to doing so now.'
He ate the fish.

Apparently, she'd been napping in class. 'Did you mention this at lunch?' She set down her wine.

'What do you mean, did I mention it? The reason we're together tonight is because you agreed to stand in for Tina.'

His tone conveyed his meaning well — he possessed zero personal interest in her. If not for this weekend with the Willoughbys, Justin Kane wouldn't grant her a second glance.

Her chest pinched, and she cleared her throat. So she wasn't Justin's type. No biggie. She didn't want a relationship right now, anyway. She'd had it with men and their games.

'I understand I'm playing your girlfriend,' she replied calmly. 'Is it really necessary to use a fake name? I'm sorry, I didn't get that from what you said at lunch.'

'I said I needed a replacement for Tina.'

'Yes, but I didn't realize you meant I had to pretend to *be* Tina. I thought you needed a generic stand-in lover, not a specific name brand.'

His gaze narrowed. 'You're backing out?'

'No. I wouldn't do that.' And risk losing his account? Not a chance. Besides, she'd already agreed to help him, and she wasn't in the habit of breaking her word.

His forehead smoothed. 'Look, I'm no expert at lying, but Nathan knows Tina's name. He expects to meet Tina Johnston — no one else. Well, and me, of course.'

Magee smiled. She'd rarely witnessed Justin Kane's sense of humor in action. That he could make light of the situation relieved her misgivings a tad.

'Aw, honey, do you know what this means?' In her best imitation of a love-struck love bunny, she batted her eyelashes. 'We just had our first fight.'

Justin chuckled. 'That's where you're wrong ... Tina. We don't disagree often, but when we do — '

'Ka-boom?'

'In a million pieces.'

'Like today?'

'Pretty much. Except usually we're sweating the small stuff. Usually something I can pick up on, and too often something I've done wrong, according to Tina. But the breakup this morning came out of nowhere. She blindsided me.' He leaned back in his chair, eyebrows hoisting in the same flabbergasted expression Magee had seen on Brent Doyle when she'd caught the worm three-timing her on New Year's Eve.

An eerie sense of déjà vu crawled over her. Neglecting her half-eaten meal, she reached for her wine. 'Let me see if I have this straight. *She* broke up with you.'

Justin nodded.

'Would you mind explaining why? Normally, I wouldn't ask, but if I'm supposed to be Tina — '

'What does one thing have to do with

55

the other? I don't want you to approach this weekend from the standpoint that you're ticked off at me. The idea is to portray a happy couple, to project an image of stability.'

'It would still help me to understand her reasons for the breakup. Everyone has their sore spots, Justin. I don't want to scrape yours by saying or doing something wrong. The more I know about Tina, the more I can prevent that from happening.'

'Okay.' His face fell into the hangdog lines of a man who felt guilty but didn't think he should. 'Tina wants to get married, and I don't.'

Magee's mind spun. *Wow.* If Tina had blindsided him with that understandable and not uncommon goal, then either Justin Kane and Tina Johnston had shared the lousiest communication skills in history — or Justin was a commitment-phobe like Brent.

'Do you love her?' she asked.

'No. For what it's worth, I don't think she loves me.'

'You don't *think?* Don't you know?'

'The subject never came up.'

'I see.' Magee resumed eating. The flaky salmon tasted like foam packing peanuts in her mouth. 'How long were you dating?'

'It would have been six months this weekend.'

Plenty of time for any sane person to fall in love. But Magee zipped her lips. A smart account executive wouldn't jeopardize her client relationship by telling Justin that if she were the Queen of England she'd confer him a snake-hood.

And she had to spend the next three days pretending to be the guy's lover?

She downed her wine. A moment later, the waiter materialized and topped up Justin's glass *first.*

Magee ground her teeth. A fiendish urge to trial-run her new identity whipped out of nowhere and pummeled the wiser option to remain silent.

'I'm Tina Johnston,' she informed the waiter as the young man took her empty glass and poured. 'I want to get married, but my boyfriend won't have it.' She flicked her hand toward Justin.

The waiter's gaze ping-ponged between them. 'Uh, congratulations?'

Justin let loose a belly laugh.

Magee glared at him. This wasn't funny!

The waiter's hands shook as he lowered Magee's glass. He must have inhaled a massive whiff of Possessed, because his lips screwed together as if he held his breath.

Face burning, she reached for the stem of her glass. Their hands collided. The glass tipped. Pinot gris sailed over her plate and splashed her dress.

Magee shrieked as the chilled wine plastered the silk to her breasts. Nipples puckering, she gaped at Justin. *Why now, God? Why, why?*

She wanted to melt into the chair and die.

Their practice date had disintegrated into the date from hell.

3

Shit! Justin leapt off his chair.

The waiter dive-bombed Magee with a serving cloth. 'Sorry, ma'am!' The kid swiped the cloth way too close to the drenched fabric clinging to Magee's obviously braless breasts.

Her round, high, perky breasts.

Mind out of the gutter, Kane.

Rescuing the toppled wineglass with one hand, Justin snatched the cloth from the waiter with the other. 'I'll take that.'

'But — but — '

'She's *my* fiancée.' He backed in front of her chair, shielding her from the bug-eyed waiter.

Behind him, Magee's voice clipped, 'Oh, now you *want* to get married?'

'Only long enough to save you from being manhandled, sweetheart.' Glowering at the waiter — and any diners who dared glance their way — Justin dangled the cloth backward.

Magee's quick tug alerted him to let go.

'I believe the correct term is waiter-handled,' she muttered as the guy scurried off.

Justin turned. She pressed the large cloth to her chest. The white wine seeped through the fabric, staining it like a Rorschach-test inkblot.

'He was only trying to help.' Lower lip protruding, she touched the cloth to the damp fabric outlining her nipples. 'You didn't have to bite off his head.'

A middle-aged lecher sat with a pinch-mouthed woman at a nearby table. The man practically slobbered all over himself gawking at Magee.

Justin hunkered beside her chair, blocking the idiot's view. *Show over, jackass.*

'Was I rude?' he asked.

'Yes.' Again, she pressed the cloth to her dress.

Justin's throat squeezed. The musky

scent of Possessed, curiously not so overpowering combined with pinot gris and the tangy ocean air, curled and floated around him.

Around her.

Around them.

'Sorry. Animal instinct.'

'It's okay.' She looked up.

'You know,' he said in a soft voice meant to tease, 'I've always enjoyed wet T-shirt contests . . . although usually the contestants lack the creativity to bathe in wine and perfume.'

She blushed. 'The sprayer stuck. On the perfume bottle. I tried washing off the scent, but then you arrived. I hoped if I didn't say anything, you wouldn't notice.'

He smiled. 'I noticed.'

'I smell awful.'

'I wouldn't say that. You smell unique.' His gaze held hers for a body-buzzing moment before she glanced away.

'Thanks, but I don't *feel* unique. My dinner's swimming in wine, my dress could keep a dry cleaner busy for a month, and everyone is staring at me. I feel like a major dufus. I need to get out of here.'

'I'll lend you my jacket.' He lifted the wispy shawl thing off her shoulders. 'This needs cleaning, too.' He folded the wine-sprinkled garment into a small rectangle and tucked it into the inside chest pocket of his sports jacket. He removed the jacket and held it for her.

'Thanks,' Magee said as she put it on. The jacket dwarfed her, the long sleeves flopping over her fingers.

Ignoring the stares of the other diners, she pushed up the sleeves and retrieved her purse, then turned and gazed at him as if to say, Let's go.

Justin had to hand it to her. She might be a walking disaster area, but she carried herself with aplomb.

Now if only he could convince her to take that self-assured woman to Whistler and leave the bumbling bombshell he'd just discovered at home.

Justin's sports jacket hung on Magee like something from the wardrobe of Frankenstein's monster. The padded shoulders extended beyond her upper arms, and the hem grazed her bare legs below her admittedly short dress. Judging from the curious stares of the arriving diners as she waited near the restaurant entrance while Justin spoke with the manager, she looked as out of place as the movie monster would at a tea party.

Yep, a couple of bolts sprouting from her neck and she'd be set.

Finally, he said goodnight to the manager and ushered her to the blissfully pedestrian-free sidewalk.

'I really wish you hadn't done that.' She crossed her arms, securing the jacket lapels over her dress.

'What? Held the door for you?' He grinned.

'No.' She wanted him to take her seriously, not think of her as a

63

one-woman sideshow. 'Insist the restaurant pay for my dry cleaning.'

'I didn't insist. It was the manager's idea. I accepted on your behalf.'

'*I* spilled the wine, Justin.'

'The waiter did.'

'I bumped his hand.'

'And he bumped yours. Call it a mutual bumping. You were standing close enough to the manager. You could have spoken up if you'd wanted.'

'I tried! You kept interrupting.'

'I had to. The Dock isn't a fast-food burger joint, Magee. The manager has a reputation to maintain. How would it look to the other customers if he didn't offer you compensation? As a businessman, I did him a favor letting him pick up the tab.'

Business. Right. Magee nodded. Tonight was about business. She'd do well to keep her reasons for agreeing to their practice date in mind. When her father returned from vacation in ten days, she wanted to be able to tell him that Justin had signed the deal with

64

Nathan Willoughby. Maybe then she'd believe she deserved the promotion her dad had conceived as the next logical step in his desire to have her join and eventually succeed him in the management of the agency.

As matters stood, she felt about as competent as a trained monkey. *Less* competent, considering the various fiascoes she'd found herself embroiled in lately. She couldn't even dance for the organ grinder without tripping over her feet these days.

All that was about to change, starting with her dealings with Justin.

She repositioned her delicate chain-link purse strap on her Frankenstein-esque shoulder. 'Where do we go from here?'

'I'll drive you home.' Justin extracted the valet parking chit from his front pants pocket.

Magee shook her head. 'Why would I want to go home?'

'This is a tough one. Give me a minute. Because you spilled wine on your dress?'

'Ah ha!' She pointed at him. 'You said the waiter spilled the wine.'

'Foiled again. However, if I remember correctly, I did permit you half the blame.'

Magee smiled. Justin had taken the wine disaster in stride. Maybe he wasn't quite the snake she'd assumed when he'd mentioned his aversion to marriage.

Or did that aversion only apply to marriage with Tina Johnston?

As if it were any of her business, and she really shouldn't pry, but —

Focus, Magee, focus.

'You did, and I'm grateful,' she said in a light vein mirroring his. 'I'm not about to run away now. I wanted to leave The Dock, but how will I learn about you and Tina if you take me home?'

'We'll cram there.'

And place herself in the position of being alone with him after she'd displayed her wares, so to speak, to his probing gaze not ten minutes ago?

'That's all right,' she said in her best

no-problem tone. 'Let's walk on the beach. I love the ocean at night.' As did dozens of other Vancouverites, she noted with a glance at the expanse of sand, grass, and full-leafed trees bordering English Bay beyond the crawling traffic of Beach Avenue.

Justin's gaze dropped to the sports jacket she wore. 'You want to walk the beach in a wet dress?'

'The warm air will dry it. And I have your coat.' She tugged the lapels. *Fake it until you make it.*

He paused. 'You're sure?'

She nodded. Sure-as-shooting sure she shouldn't let herself be alone with him. Heat pooled in her lower body at the thought of attempting another practice kiss in the stairwell.

Taking him back to her apartment was *not* a good idea.

★ ★ ★

'The beach it is.' Justin pocketed the parking chit and accompanied Magee toward the crosswalk. He counted himself lucky she'd agreed to continue the practice date at all. He wouldn't begrudge her a walk on the beach, although he'd have to see what he could do about keeping them to the grassy area so gritty sand wouldn't wedge between her toes.

Hopefully, if the gods of subterfuge smiled on them, the stroll would help Magee unwind. He'd never seen her so jumpy. The prospect of masquerading as Tina — of pretending she and Justin were a couple — had tied her in knots. He wanted her to feel comfortable with the idea.

To that end, he offered her his hand. She hesitated, gaze wary as a startled doe's. Then, smile uncertain, she pushed up the sleeve of the sports jacket and slipped her hand in his.

Justin returned her smile as they crossed the road. Magee's hand was smaller than Tina's, the nails short yet still smooth with polish, her fingers slim and ring-less. Warmth radiated from her palm, infusing him with a vibrant energy he'd come to associate with her. He'd never experienced the same sensation with Tina.

Maybe his ex had been right to dump him.

For several minutes, they walked the grassy, leaf-strewn area of beach without speaking while misty streaks of deep orange and a pink resembling the roses in his mother's garden painted the sky with the shimmering glow that preceded Vancouver's stunning ocean sunsets. The gradually cooling evening breeze drifted off English Bay as seagulls cawed and swooped down to the wet sand. Sailboats bobbed on the water, and, in the distance, anchored freighters waited to approach the piers in Burrard Inlet and unload.

Soon similar freighters would carry Willoughby Bikes cargo bound for the new warehouse and distribution center Justin had checked out this afternoon — and his long-anticipated expansion plans for the CycleMania chain of bike stores would be a go.

Soon. He could almost taste the achievement on this tongue. Only after attaining his business goals would he consider the possibility of marriage. He'd offer his future wife and children the same full-hearted devotion he intended to put into building his business over the next five years. No child of his would feel neglected and unloved, like Justin and his younger brothers had. He'd make sure of that. To a kid, a workaholic father felt like having no father at all.

But first things first. Namely, signing the deal with Willoughby Bikes. Which meant convincing Nathan that every facet of Justin's life was under control . . . which, in turn, hinged on the acting abilities of the female whirlwind walking beside him.

His gut clenched. A whirlwind could do a hell of a lot of damage.

'Look!' the whirlwind in question said. 'A popcorn vendor. Want some?'

Releasing his hand, she raced toward the cart parked near the sand.

By the time Justin caught up to her, she'd paid for the popcorn.

He patted her arm. 'My wallet's in the jacket. Grab it for me, and I'll pay you back.'

'What is this, the 1950s? You bought dinner, I'll get dessert.'

'You didn't finish your meal.'

'Don't remind me.' She glanced at a passing teenage boy staring at the sports jacket skimming her thighs. She beamed a two-hundred-watt smile at the kid, and he jumped, face reddening, before scooting off.

'Works like a charm,' she murmured. Her gaze returned to Justin's. 'Tonight is about business, remember? I'll expense the popcorn.'

Yeah, he believed she'd write off a bag of popcorn. However, he didn't want to come across like some Neanderthal who couldn't stand to have a woman pay, so he dropped the subject.

She dug into the popcorn, then held

the bag for him. He scooped out a handful.

'Okay,' she said as they munched and walked on the hard-packed area of beach. 'Let's review what I know so far. We're lovers, we've dated six months, my name's Tina Johnston . . . ' Her hand stilled in the popcorn bag. 'What's my middle name?'

'Uh.' Justin searched his mind for the answer — and came up with a big, fat blank.

'You don't know your girlfriend's middle name?' Magee asked as if he'd broken dating rule number one. Whatever that was.

'*Ex*-girlfriend.' So what if he didn't know Tina's middle name? She didn't know his, either. 'Do we need to get that specific? I can't see Nathan asking your middle name.'

'You never know. The more details at my disposal, the better.'

She sounded like a burglar preparing to pull off a bank heist. A cute, sexy burglar with a slightly upturned nose

72

and an enticing aroma.

He shrugged. 'Use your own middle name.'

'Luanne?' She munched popcorn. 'That's bad enough with Magee, but for Tina? How about something simple like Lynn?'

'Then make it Lynn.'

'I will. Tina Lynn.' Magee chewed more popcorn. 'Yes, I like that.'

Justin chuckled. 'I'm glad . . . Luanne.'

She blasted him a look that could wither daisies. '*Magee.*'

'Tina.'

'*Tomorrow.*'

'Whatever.' She was too cute for premature name-changing, he didn't care what he'd suggested earlier.

They reached a grouping of clean, gray drift logs where the hard-packed beach gave way to loose sand. The logs, positioned by parks personnel to face the water, served as the city's West Coast version of benches.

'My favorite part of walking the

beach.' Magee removed her sandals and set them nearby, then hopped onto the largest drift log as naturally as an acrobat would the high wire.

So much for keeping her *off* the sand. At least, on the big log, she'd remain above it.

Justin grasped her free hand to steady her, and Magee methodically placed one bare foot in front of the other on the log. She held the popcorn bag away from her, maintaining her balance. Her tiny purse bobbed against her hip as she pecked her way along.

'Next question.' She glanced at him. 'How old am I?'

Good, an easy answer. 'Thirty-four.'

'I'm twenty-nine! That's a five-year difference.'

'Don't worry. No one can tell.'

Her mouth twisted in a expression that said, *Come on, dig yourself in deeper. You can do it. After all, you're male.*

He should know that expression.

74

He'd received it often enough from Tina.

'Not that you don't appear younger than Tina,' he backpedaled. 'Because you do. But she buys enough skin cream to saturate a killer whale, so she looks quite youn — uh, good, too.'

Magee laughed. 'Relax. I was teasing.'

'I knew that.' He didn't know jack. He reached into his pants pocket and withdrew a folded sheet of paper. He should have produced the list earlier, but Magee had distracted him with her enchanting whirlwind tendencies.

'What's that?' She munched more popcorn.

'A cheat sheet. Everything you always wanted to know about Tina Johnston.'

'What little you can tell me, you mean.' Magee grabbed the cheat sheet. She passed him the popcorn bag, unfolded the sheet, and scanned it. She giggled — a sound of pure delight floating on the ocean-scented air. 'Justin, I'm sorry, this is so neatly prepared it's priceless. One fact to a line, complete with dashes and color-coded ink.'

'I find it pays to be organized.' He tossed a popcorn tidbit to a seagull.

Magee stood with her bare feet braced on the drift log, reading from the sheet with gusto, 'Tina Johnston, age thirty-four, manages a clothing store on Robson. I wonder if I've shopped there? Would help if I knew the *name*. Never married,' she continued without allowing him a chance to respond. 'One sister and a brother, blah, blah, blah.' Her gaze flicked over the cheat sheet. 'Good, information on you. Justin Kane, no mention of a middle name, although I'm sure you have one. Age thirty-five, two brothers, both parents alive. Ah, here we go.' She peered at the sheet. 'Oh.'

'What?'

'Well, it says you live in a two-bedroom condo with a view of Coal Harbor. Nice, Justin. Very nice. But I need more. As Tina, I would be familiar with your living room, the color of your towels and bed sheets. What if Nathan's wife asks?'

About his bed sheets? 'I'll email another list to your cell.'

'No.' She lifted a hand. 'Digital footprints. Bad idea. With my luck — '

'Digital footprints bad. I get it.' Not really. Was she worried she'd punch the wrong speed-dial and forward the sheet to — who? 'I'll *print* a new cheat sheet and bring it along tomorrow. You'll need to keep it out of sight.'

'From the Willoughbys? Of course. I'm not stupid.'

'*Mea culpa.*'

'Apology accepted.' Her fingertips skimmed along the cheat sheet. 'List colors and furniture styles, number of bedrooms and baths. Bookshelves, the size of your TV. How about pets? It doesn't say anything here about a pet.'

'I don't have one.' He'd never owned a cat or dog. Not even a gerbil. His mother believed animals were too much bother. And his father . . . if it didn't walk and talk corporate law, Richard Kane wasn't interested.

Magee's lips pursed. 'Any plants? If you don't have pets, you must have plants.'

'Tina gave me a cactus for Valentine's Day. Does that count?'

'In a pinch.'

'Good. Because this weekend definitely qualifies.'

She smiled. A soft, slow smile that tilted her sparkling eyes.

Man. Justin's chest caved as if he'd been sucker-punched. The woman magnetized him. Why couldn't he and Magee have met several months ago? During early winter or last fall? Before he and Tina had hooked up.

Then this weekend wouldn't have to be based on a lie.

Pocketing the cheat sheet, Magee turned on the drift log. She wobbled.

'Easy.' He placed a hand on the sports jacket covering her hip.

She flinched. 'I stubbed my toe.'

Setting down the popcorn bag, Justin

bent on one knee in the sand. The big toe of Magee's left foot sported a thin red scratch courtesy of a rough knot in the log.

He caressed the scratch with his thumb. Her legs carried the fading scent of Possessed. Did the woman wear perfume *everywhere?*

He'd love to find out.

Keep it together, Kane.

He checked her toe. 'No splinters. Clean the scrape with antiseptic before you go to bed tonight, and you'll be fine.'

'Thanks.'

He should stand up now, but he really didn't want to. He couldn't resist giving her toe one last swipe of his thumb. His finger grazed the nail adorned with rich, pink polish. She drew in a breath.

Her skin felt like satin beneath his fingers. He glided his hand over her smooth, bare leg. Mouth drying, he cupped her calf.

God, she had great legs.

'Justin,' she whispered.

He looked up. She gazed down at him, eyes wide and luminous. The breeze rustled her chin-length hair around her face against the purply-pink hues of the gathering sunset.

Releasing her calf, he stood. Clasping her fingers, he held them by his sides at mid-thigh. The drift log added several centimeters to her height, bringing them face to face, his nose a shadow above hers and mouths so close their breaths mingled.

He brushed her lips with his, a feathery stroke, a caress.

'Is this our practice kiss?' she whispered against his mouth.

Practice? *Oh yeah*. Good thing she'd reminded him.

'Yes,' he murmured, recapturing her mouth. Their fingers slid together at their sides, tangling and untangling, until only their fingertips touched . . . the connection light and unbearably erotic.

Restraining a groan, he let their

fingertips slip apart. He ached to touch her, but refused to indulge himself. He ached to hold her, kiss her deeply.

He lifted his palms a hair-breadth over her upper arms, then pulled the urge inside himself and rested his hands on his thighs.

Touching her, yet not touching.

Touching her only with his mouth.

She tasted of salty popcorn . . . and a splash of wine.

He traced her lips with his tongue. Her mouth parted slightly, and she trembled. The tip of her tongue flitted out, meeting his.

And then something happened for Justin that had never happened before. The *earth* moved. Shifted. Tilted.

Magee was melting into him, then floating, floating, floating away. Floating as if she were falling backward.

And then she *was* falling.

His eyes popped open. He swung out a hand to grab her. A fistful of tweed rasped his palm as her arms flung wide. She squeaked, and he yanked her toward him. The sports jacket ripped as she crashed into his chest. He stumbled back a step.

Quickly, he regained his balance and caught her as she lurched off the log. Her right foot plunged into the popcorn bag. Paper crunched and fluffy balls of popcorn sprang out, littering the sand.

'Omigod, what happened?' Pushing away, she shook the bag off her bare foot.

'Isn't it obvious? I knocked you off your feet with my kiss.' The seagull he'd fed a few minutes ago emitted a gleeful squawk. Within seconds, five gulls pecked at the popcorn bits. Justin scattered the birds with a sweep of his hand.

'No, not that. *This.*' Magee lifted her left arm in a wing-like movement, exposing the underarm of his jacket — split through the seam.

'That must have happened when I grabbed you. Sorry.'

'Why are you sorry?' She unwound

the purse strap that had twisted around her right arm with the fall. 'I lost my balance. Now your jacket's ruined, and it's my fault.'

'Your fault? Magee, you wound me. What's more, I can't accept your position. No, I stand firm in my assertion that it was my kiss that made you fall.'

His attempt to cheer her flopped. 'I don't want to play Chip and Dale over this, Justin. I ruined the jacket. I'll get it fixed. A seamstress works in the building around the corner from the ad agency. I need to go into the office for a couple of hours tomorrow, anyway. I'll drop off your jacket at Mrs. Rubens's in the morning, then return it when we get back from Whistler.'

Chip and Dale? Had he heard her correctly? Those polite little chipmunks he watched on VHS tapes as a kid?

Justin wasn't certain he liked being compared to a chipmunk.

'Hey, don't get wrapped up about it. That jacket is two or three years old. It was bound to suffer wear and tear eventually.' *And* literally. She'd worn the sports jacket and he'd torn it.

Red spotted her cheeks. 'Justin, this was my mistake. Please allow me to fix it.'

Her lips didn't hold one trace of a smile. She was serious. Mending the sports jacket meant something to her. What, he hadn't a clue. However, he'd had enough experience with the fairer and ultra-confusing sex to realize he should back off on this point — quick.

'No sweat. Take the jacket to your seamstress.'

'Thank you.' Magee turned away, muttering, 'At least this is something I can't screw up.'

Her tone didn't exactly radiate confidence . . . or inspire it in him. Was he asking too much of her to masquerade as Tina? What had seemed a logical solution to his dilemma this morning now appeared fraught with unanticipated perils that might be alleviated given another few days of preparation and practice.

But they didn't *have* a few days. He glanced at his watch. Even if he asked Magee to stay awake all night to study — which didn't make sense, considering they both needed to be rested and alert tomorrow — they had about sixteen hours until Nathan Willoughby's plane landed and this whole crackbrained scheme set in motion.

A measly sixteen hours.

He was screwed.

4

'Monster, please stay out of my suitcase.' For the third time since Magee had rushed home from a hectic morning at the office to check her packing for Whistler, she scooped the purring cat out of the open suitcase on her bed. 'You can nap indoors until I leave, but only if you stay put.' She plopped him onto the nearest pillow.

The cat meowed, kneading the pillow. A moment later, he curled into a ball and resumed purring, as if he'd come to see things her way after all.

Magee tucked two pairs of socks into the light hiking boots Justin had suggested she bring. Her stomach looped like a jet performing stunts at the Abbotsford Airshow. If she didn't tame her anxiety, she'd regress into a walking bundle of nerves before she even met the Willoughbys. Forget about doing a good job as Tina Johnston then! She'd be fortunate to manage a decent imitation of herself.

She puffed out a breath. Why didn't she *think* before diving headlong into these disasters-waiting-to-happen? For awhile, she'd made great progress. Last summer, every decision she'd reached as an account executive had resulted in increased agency revenue. Yet, since January, her mistakes had eaten into the increases until beautiful black had depleted to alarming red.

By May, Magee couldn't abide red. Justin Kane's business had seemed the shortest route back to glossy black.

If only she hadn't lied to Justin in order to land his account. But she *had* lied, and now she had to deal with the fallout . . . or risk the double-whammy of losing another client and facing her father's disappointment when he discovered her fib.

Her father would definitely be disappointed. In her, and maybe also in himself for believing she could do her job without backsliding into her lifelong tendency to commit blunders. The unscheduled phone call she'd received from him at work this morning still pricked her conscience. He'd said he was only checking in. Instead, she'd felt like he was checking up on her ability to manage the agency without him. His encouraging words when she'd said she might have a chance to meet Nathan Willoughby over the next few days had made her feel doubly worse.

She stuffed the hiking boots into the suitcase and wadded her bikini into a mesh corner pocket. On top of everything else today, she'd endured another of Patti Slotnik's subtle smirks. Obviously, the woman believed the worst of her. To accommodate the Whistler trip, Magee had postponed the Client Services staff meeting until Monday. She hadn't provided an explanation for her absence. How could she risk the truth leaking out before she had a chance to explain her actions to her father?

Everyone except Patti had accepted Magee's announcement with the same respect they would grant her dad.

Magee could live with the woman's attitude for now. Pulling off her role as Tina had to take precedence.

'Isn't that right, Monster?' she asked the cat.

His sleepy amber eyes slit open. Yawning, he stretched a furry gray paw.

'Good, I'm glad you agree.' Magee folded a nightgown into the suitcase, then intercepted the cat as he slid like melting ice cream off the pillow to within clawing distance of the suitcase's tempting top flap. 'Oh no, you don't.'

She repositioned the cat on the pillow and hurried to the bathroom for her makeup pouch. When she returned, Monster sat smack in the middle of the suitcase. Cat hair sprinkled over her packed clothes as he licked his paw and cleaned his whiskers.

'That's it!' Magee chucked the toiletry bag on the bed. She lifted the cat in mid-yowl and lugged him to the kitchen. Placing him on the shingled roof below the gable window, she said, 'Sorry, boy. See you next week.'

Monster meowed and strutted toward the tall cedar shrub at the roof edge, his fluffy tail poking the air.

As Magee pulled shut the window lever against the warm summer afternoon, an ice-blue van sporting the CycleMania logo parked at the sidewalk. Justin climbed out, looking relaxed and casually sexy in khakis and a buttery-cream golf shirt. Her pulse raced. He glanced toward the window, mouth curving in a smile that evoked breath-stealing images of beaches, sunsets, and seductive kisses in her mind.

For a second, her hand remained glued to the lever while her whole body blushed. *Mercy.* Last night might have qualified as the date from hell, but Justin Kane kissed like pure heaven. No wonder she'd lost her balance on the drift log.

He advanced to the walkway leading

to the house. Scurrying to her bedroom, Magee swept her suitcase relatively free of cat hairs, tossed in her makeup pouch, and zipped the case. She checked the apartment lights and locks before beating Justin to the landing outside her door.

Setting the suitcase on the worn wood floor, she inhaled a deep breath. *Tina Johnston, here I come.* For the weekend, she *was* Tina.

Justin rounded the corner of the staircase.

'Hi.' Magee smiled.

'Hi, yourself. You look great.' His gaze drifted over her sundress.

'Thanks,' she responded gaily. Last night was a foggy memory. Or, she needed it to be. She wanted the first day of the rest of their fake relationship to get off to a good start.

'I wrote up the second cheat sheet,' Justin announced with the pride of a school kid who'd remembered his homework. 'Used a pen. No digital footprints.' He tapped his skull.

Magee's stomach knotted. In her rush to reschedule her work week, the cheat sheets had completely slipped her mind. 'Uh, did you email the first sheet to your cell?'

'No. Why? Digital footprints, remember? It's on my laptop at home, though.'

She chewed her bottom lip. 'Did you include the information from the first sheet on the second one?'

'No,' Justin said again. 'Was I supposed to?'

'I don't think so. Not that I can recall specifying . . . ' Her humiliation upon ruining his sports jacket had rendered much of the previous evening a blur. She'd just wanted to go home. To his credit, he'd obliged her without complaint.

'Then what's the problem?' he asked.

'It appears I left the first cheat sheet in your jacket pocket, and I took the jacket to Mrs. Rubens this morning. We can drive there first. I need those crib notes.' She couldn't begin the weekend with another snafu.

He rubbed his chin. 'We don't have time to go downtown. I can't chance the Willoughbys coming out of Customs early with no one there to greet them.' He withdrew the second cheat sheet from his pants pocket. 'I remember details from the first sheet. We'll rehash them on the way to the airport. You can make notes on this sheet while I drive.' He handed her the sheet. 'Do you have a pen?'

'In my purse.' Magee unfolded the sheet. The first line of Justin's neat handwriting proclaimed: *middle name, Matthew*.

She smiled. 'Justin Matthew. How sweet.'

'Tina Lynn.' He winked. 'How *you*.'

She chuckled. 'Thanks.'

'For calling you Tina? That's a switch from last night.'

You know, she really liked this man when he unstuffed his shirt. 'For not getting into a tizzy about the first cheat sheet,' she said as he picked up her suitcase and motioned her ahead of him down the stairs.

His footsteps sounded close behind her. 'Considering you're helping me out for the next week, I figure I shouldn't act like a total ass.'

'Smart thinking.' *Wait a minute.* As they reached the front porch, she faced him. 'The next week?' she echoed. 'We're returning from Whistler on Sunday.'

'Yes, but the Willoughbys are staying in Vancouver until next Friday. I have to show them the stores and tour them around the local mountain biking trails. Remember?'

Oh yeah, she recalled him mentioning something along those lines during yesterday's ill-fated lunch. However, he'd neglected to clarify one mucho-important detail.

'Next Friday — that's eight days from now. You're telling me I have to pretend to be Tina for the next eight days?' She'd thought three nights in Whistler sounded rough.

He patted her shoulder. 'It's not like

94

you'll be on-call twenty-four/seven. You have a job — as Tina, I mean. The Willoughbys realize you'll be back at work on Monday.' He strode toward the van. 'Coming?'

Did she have a choice? She scurried to catch up. *Good little duckling.*

Storing her suitcase behind the rows of seats, Justin said, 'I *will* need you to play Tina in the evenings from time to time. Nathan and his wife want to sample the restaurants, maybe take in a show. Tina loves opera, so I bought tickets to *La Bohème*. You know, before . . . '

His ex became his ex.

Someone shoot me. Surely a quick death would be preferable to this slow torture.

'I'll clear my schedule,' Magee mumbled. Not a difficult task. She'd adhered to a strict no-dating diet since her failed relationship with Brent.

Justin opened the passenger door for her.

She placed her hand on the armrest,

but didn't climb in. 'Justin, I'm having trouble absorbing the finer points of your plan. I need you to tell me, is there anything else — anything at all — not covered on the cheat sheets I need to know about my role before we leave?'

His gaze settled on her. 'No . . . maybe . . . okay, yes, there's something.'

'What?'

'Tina doesn't wear underwear.'

'She does now!' Face flaming, Magee ducked into the van.

★ ★ ★

Justin sat discussing business with the Willoughbys at the long, mess-hall-style table in his parents' cabin. However, despite the several hours that had passed since he and Magee had picked up the English couple from Vancouver International, Magee flitted like a hyperactive hummingbird around the cabin kitchen. Cupboards clacked and canister lids clattered as she prepared the evening's second pot of tea.

Justin tracked her movements with furtive glances. 'Tina' clearly suffered from information overload. During the drive to the airport, and then later, while they'd waited for the Willoughbys to emerge from Customs, he and Magee had reviewed each item on the second cheat sheet multiple times. They'd also rehearsed the details from the first sheet forgotten in his torn sports jacket. He'd quizzed Magee, reassured her, and teased her — all in a vain effort to calm her nerves.

If anything, Magee was even more frazzled now that they'd returned from dinner in Whistler Village than when Justin had arrived at her apartment this afternoon.

No more jokes about underwear.

The comment had sprung from his fantasies about what she might or might *not* be wearing beneath her sky-blue sundress. Since the wine incident, he'd thought about little else.

He should have kept his trap shut. His accomplice had so much on her plate, she was about to drop it — or the teapot she clutched, to be more accurate.

'More tea, Nathan?' Magee approached the table with the fresh pot of an English blend Justin had bought at a Vancouver specialty shop. She balanced the bulky pottery monstrosity with her pot-holder-protected left hand. Her right hand gripped the thick rattan handle arching over the teapot lid.

'Thanks, if it's no bother,' Nathan answered in the crisp London accent Justin had heard on the phone but couldn't quite match with Nathan's white-blond buzz cut and the small bike wheel tattoo beneath his left ear, never mind the Internet photos corroborating the younger man's appearance. 'But please, Tina, do sit down. We'd rather chat to you a bit longer than have you serve us all evening. Isn't that so, Kate?'

'Of course. Come on, Tina, have a seat.'

Kathryn, a vivacious brunette in her mid-twenties, had taken an instant liking to Magee — as Tina. During the trip up the mountain, Kathryn had asked so many questions about 'Tina's' family and job that Justin had feared his fake lover would keel over from the exertion of trying to answer them all. He'd contributed when possible. However, every time he'd interrupted the women's conversation, he'd risked appearing overbearing. Coming across as in control of his life and business was one thing. A positive spin. An image he wanted to promote. Overbearing, on the other hand, might be viewed in a negative light. Not only from Kathryn's perspective, but Nathan's, too.

The fact was, Justin couldn't do 'in control' with his pseudo-girlfriend rattling around the Willoughbys like the lid on the overfull teapot. If he wanted his plan to succeed, he needed Magee to calm down.

And he did want the plan to work. Of that, he had no doubt. He had to believe in Magee. After all, she hadn't convinced him to move his business to Sinclair Advertising by making an amateurish presentation. She'd argued a compelling case for working with a smaller, more attentive agency rather than the impersonal behemoth he'd been using, and he'd capitulated.

A no-brainer once he'd factored in her passion for mountain biking.

'Yes, Tina, please *join us*,' Justin heavily hinted as she refilled Nathan's cup. A drop of hot tea splashed over the cup rim and pooled on the younger man's saucer.

'Oops, sorry.' Magee wiped the splash with the potholder. As her fingers tightened on the handle, her wrist bent at an awkward angle. Her forearm trembled.

Magee stepped away from Nathan. 'Kathryn, how about you? More tea?'

'Another cup sounds smashing, thank you.' Kathryn slid over her cup on the table. 'And sorry, but let's put a stop to this Nathan and Kathryn business, shall we? It's Kate and Nate, like we said at dinner. We're all friends now, right?'

'R-right,' Magee stammered. 'Kate and . . . and Nate.' Her panicky gaze flew to Justin.

Relax, he mouthed.

Gnawing her lip, she refilled Kate's teacup, then reclaimed her seat beside him on the bench.

'Take it easy,' Justin murmured in her ear. Burrowing his nose into her neck lover-style, he whispered, 'You're doing great.' He clasped her hand beneath the tabletop and entwined it to rest with his upon his thigh.

The gesture didn't calm her, like he'd stupidly hoped. Her hand tensed and popped free of his, as quick as a mouse escaping a faulty trap.

Justin drew in a short breath. Nate, sitting shoulder-to-shoulder with Kate across the table, couldn't precisely *see* Justin and 'Tina' holding hands, but that was beside the point. He was striving for believability. Didn't Magee understand that?

He skated his hand along the bench

and captured hers again. She cooperated, her hand relaxing to some extent. His thumb itched to glide over her smooth, warm skin. Instead, he slipped her a thankful-disguised-as-loving smile and resumed discussing business with Nate.

They'd progressed to an animated discussion about Whistler's mountain biking trails when — *pop!* — Magee's hand scuttled free again.

What the hell?

Talking to Nate, Justin reached for her hand. Magee continued chatting with Kate and deftly evaded his grasp.

Damn it.

Justin grabbed. Magee yanked. He tugged, and she warred.

Gritting his teeth and struggling not to show it, Justin made a final play for his prize. Overshooting, he captured a handful of silky thigh. Soft, yet toned. *Incredible.*

Stiffening, she shoved his hand off her leg. Hers fell onto the bench seat and stayed there.

After a moment, Justin grasped her hand again. Her fingers twitched, then settled. He smiled. *Ladies and gentlemen, we have a winner.*

Kate and Nate exchanged an amused glance, and Justin held his breath. Had they picked up on the tension flowing between him and Magee? They'd better consider it the sexual variety!

'We might want to save the biking trails for Saturday,' he said, addressing the group. 'That leaves tomorrow to explore Whistler or do some easy hiking. Swimming, shopping, zip lines — whatever suits you.'

'Shopping?' Kate's dark eyebrows bobbed. 'Ooh, I'd hate that, wouldn't I?'

'Quite.' Nate kissed her cheek. 'If I'm to be up to such a strenuous activity, I'd best have an early night. We had some long days in California, and I'm shattered.'

'Shattered?' Magee asked, her hand squirming inside Justin's.

'Exhausted,' Kate explained. She

checked her watch. 'Yes, it's quarter to ten already. What do you say, Justin? Do you mind if we turn in?'

'Not at all.' He'd tuck them in if they wanted. He'd do damn near anything to ensure the success of this weekend. He'd like to believe his fake girlfriend felt the same.

'Wait!' Magee leapt from the bench seat as if his hand had grown teeth. 'I'll join you.'

Nate grinned. 'Thanks for the offer, but Kate's more than enough for one chap.'

Magee's eyes widened. 'That's not what I meant. Oh, you're joking, of course. Heh-heh.' Slapping her chest, she released another atrocious imitation of a laugh. 'What I meant to say was I'd like to go to bed, too.'

Oh yeah? And leave Justin sitting all alone downstairs looking like the cat who didn't know what to do with a bowl of cream?

I don't think so.

'Not without me, sweetcheeks.' He

stood and wrapped an arm around her, pinning her to his side in a desperate bid to keep her from jumping out of her skin.

* * *

Magee unpacked her suitcase into an empty dresser drawer. Justin stood on the opposite side of the double bed, hands on his hips as he lectured her. 'The plan was to stay downstairs until *after* Kate and Nate went to sleep.'

'I know that,' she returned in the hushed voices they'd employed since saying goodnight to the Willoughbys and closing the door on 'their' bedroom. 'Don't you think I know that?'

'Then what happened?'

He sounded like a coach with laryngitis reaming out a player. Magee shoved her hiking boots beneath the chair holding her suitcase. 'I learned some plans work better in theory than practice.' She tossed her socks into a drawer.

He stared at her. 'What does that mean? We discussed the sleeping arrangements over and over on the way to the airport. The Willoughbys get the master bedroom while we pretend to share this one. They'd go to bed, we'd stay downstairs. Watch a movie. Play cards. Something. After an hour, we'd come up. You'd sleep in this room and I'd take the bunk room. What's simpler?'

What wasn't? Or was Justin so adept at playing games that the pretense didn't faze him?

'If I didn't have to use Tina's name, for one thing,' she whispered. 'If I didn't have to keep racking my brains for the information on the cheat sheet, and that sheet, when I most need it, is stashed deep inside my purse where the Willoughbys can't see it. If I could have come here as your date or platonic friend instead of as your lover.' She stuffed two T-shirts into the drawer. 'I don't know about you, but to me those scenarios sound *much* simpler.'

'And they have no bearing on the matter, because I do need you to play Tina. Why dwell on something we can't change?'

'Because!' Glancing at the wall separating their room from the Willoughbys', she lowered her voice. 'If not for this lover bit, we wouldn't have to sneak between rooms. And we could have been spared that thumb-wrestling bout downstairs.'

Justin crossed his arms. 'That's what rattled you. The holding hands,' he continued in his husky near-whisper.

'Yes, the holding hands. The kissing at dinner. The . . . snuggling.' The constant barrage of affected affection had distracted her to no end. It was a miracle she'd managed to pull off her performance.

If she had pulled it off. She wasn't convinced the Willoughbys couldn't see straight through her.

'You kept *touching* me.'

A muscle in Justin's jaw flexed. 'That was the idea.'

'Granted, but you went overboard.'

'And that bothered you.'

'Yes.' Although it hadn't bothered her in the way he might think. A man's touch hadn't aroused her to such a degree since she'd dated Brent.

Actually, she hadn't experienced the sweeping, tilt-her-world sensations Justin elicited in her *while* she'd dated Brent.

A shadow flitted over Justin's face. 'You don't want me to touch you. A tall order, considering the circumstances, but I'll restrain myself.'

He had it so wrong. She did want him to touch her. She wanted him, period — lunatic that she was.

Her emerging feelings for Justin — as clear as creamed coffee and about as appealing to someone who took hers black, two sugars — would only mess with her equilibrium and wreak havoc in an already crazy situation. Better to let him believe she'd rather suntan in hell than endure another episode like tonight's.

'Thank you.' Maintaining a low

voice, she continued unpacking. 'While we're talking about the Willoughbys, I have to say that they're not anything like I expected. And, yes, I googled them, but still. I mean, Kate and Nate? Not mentioned anywhere, and even I think that's corny. He can't be a day older than me, and she looks younger.'

Justin didn't reply. Magee glanced over her shoulder. Torso stiff, he unpacked his suitcase into a small dresser on the other side of the bed.

'Don't get me wrong,' she said. 'I like them, but they're pretty laid back. Would it really be so awful if they found out I'm not Tina?'

His gaze whipped around. 'What?'

'I think we should tell them.'

'Are you nuts?'

Obviously, he thought so.

'Nathan's laid-back attitude has nothing to do with the signing of the deal,' Justin half-whispered. 'This trip is a vacation for him and his wife as well as a chance to do business. He should feel relaxed. Learning we're pulling the wool over his eyes won't help get him there.'

'Okay, I see your point.' It would be difficult to miss, considering he'd rammed it down her throat. 'But I feel like I've been misled. That Nate is combining business with pleasure isn't the issue. Whatever happened to your spiel about longstanding British traditions, the stiff upper lip, and so on?'

'Stability in business and relationships,' Justin quoted from yesterday's lunch. 'The philosophy still applies.' He unpacked a pair of gray sweatpants and tossed them on the bed. 'Look, Nate might not fit your idea of an English gentleman. He doesn't fit mine. But he values honor and commitment, and he'll relay his impressions of me and CycleMania to his father once he's back in London. Frederick Willoughby *is* of the old guard, and Frederick has the final say on this deal.'

Cut and dried. Pure business. Had Justin compartmentalized his relationship with Tina as easily as he did his career?

'The end justifies the means,' she murmured.

Justin's slate-blue gaze penetrated her from across the room. 'For me, it has to. Signing this deal with Willoughby Bikes will give me the edge I need to open more stores. Expanding CycleMania is the most important thing in my life.'

He couldn't have provided a more revealing answer about his apparently puddle-deep feelings for Tina if Magee had asked him point blank.

'I understand that, and I won't back out. The situation's still hard for me. Put yourself in my place. You don't have to pretend to be someone you're not.'

'Yes, but I do need to pretend you're Tina. Believe me, Miss Sinclair, you're nothing like her.'

'Why? Because I wear underwear?'

A laugh popped out of him. 'No, because you're real. A little wacky sometimes, but real.'

Magee hesitated. She wasn't as real as he assumed. However, confessing her

111

lack of mountain biking skills at this late stage didn't seem the wisest choice. So she smiled, hoping she didn't look brainless. 'Should we change?'

Nodding, he retrieved his sweats. 'I'll use the bathroom.'

'No, that's okay, unless you really have to use the bathroom.' The Willoughbys' room boasted an en suite bath, but the shared upstairs bathroom sat at the far end of the hall. 'We're supposed to be lovers, and lovers wouldn't change in separate rooms.' Lovers wouldn't sleep in separate rooms, either, but Magee could only handle so much role-playing in one night.

Justin shrugged. 'Your call.' He whipped off his shirt faster than she could think, *Oh my gosh! What gorgeous pectorals!*

'Not in front of me!' she whispered hoarsely. 'Turn around!'

He turned. Heart pounding, Magee searched her suitcase. Dismissing the lacy chemise and satin robe she favored in warm weather, she snatched the long flannel nightgown she'd packed in case the heavy rains the Vancouver area had experienced a week ago returned. She'd rather sweat like a pig and look like a frump than give Justin any reason to think she'd changed her mind about the touching.

'Are you still turned?' she asked.

'Yep.'

After his little striptease, she didn't trust him. Glancing over her shoulder, she sucked in a dizzying breath. The top half of Justin's naked butt presented itself to her as he pulled on the gray sweats, his head bowed.

Heat flooded her. *Gluteus maxi-my-my*. Very bite-able.

Averting her gaze, she dragged off her sundress. Keeping on her bra and panties in a salute to modesty, she tugged on the granny nightgown and speed-buttoned the bodice. 'I'm done. Are you?'

'Yep.'

She faced him, gaining an unavoid-able eyeful of his sculpted chest above the low-riding sweats. His gaze drifted over her buttercup-dotted nightgown. Smiling, he ambled across the bedroom. Her breath caught with each slow, deliberate step.

He stopped in front of her, so close she could touch him if she dared. His gaze dipped to her nightgown . . . right above her breasts.

His hand lifted. Extending a finger, he grazed a button. 'You missed one,' he whispered, his voice as thick and soft as the flannel brushing her skin.

She looked down. Her buttons marched like drunken soldiers up her chest, popped into buttonholes willy-nilly. Twisted and jumbled. All askew.

Well, what do you know? Another mess.

Couldn't she handle one virginal nightgown?

Spinning around, she re-buttoned the bodice. When she faced Justin again, he'd cupped his ear against the shared wall.

'All's quiet on the Willoughby front,' he murmured.

'That doesn't mean they're asleep. They could be . . . busy.'

His eyebrows waggled. 'In that case, we don't have anything to worry about.'

'I guess not.' Unless she counted her very real and dangerous attraction to him.

'Time to make my move.' He fiddled with his watch. 'I'll set my alarm for five a.m. and sneak back in here before Kate and Nate get up. That way, it will look like you and I spent the night together.' He pressed a hand on the mattress. 'You should be comfortable. This is a new bed. I tried it in the spring, and it felt great.'

In the spring? Magee swallowed. Now there was a snag she hadn't considered. Sleeping in a bed Justin had recently used would be difficult enough with visions of his sugar-plum body dancing in her head. However, using the bed in which he might have

115

entertained his ex bordered on the . . . *icky*.

No way would she sleep in a bed he'd shared with Tina.

5

Justin's co-conspirator looked sick. What had upset Magee now? His intention to return to the bedroom at dawn?

'I already said I'll cut down on the touching,' he said, 'but Nate might grow suspicious if we don't provide the illusion of sharing a room. That doesn't mean I plan on climbing into your bed at five.' Actually, the idea intrigued him. Big time. However, Magee had provided several indications that the mere prospect of his touch creeped her out. 'There's a sleeping bag on the closet shelf. I'll make a bed on the floor before I go. When I come in tomorrow, I promise I won't wake you, and I promise I won't peek beneath the covers while you're sleeping. Furthermore, if it helps, I promise that, from this point forward, I won't so much as peck you on the cheek in front of, behind, or to the left or right of either of the Willoughbys without your implied or expressed permission.' He might sound like his father dictating a legal document with that last bit, but he'd covered his bases. Magee couldn't throw a curveball past him if she tried.

'It's not the touching,' she stage-whispered. 'Although I appreciate your, um, efforts not to. It's just, if it's all the same to you, I'd like to switch rooms.'

So she was one hell of a pitcher. '*You* would,' he whispered back.

She nodded. 'Instead of you.'

'Magee, those bunk beds are old and lumpy.'

'I don't care.'

He shook his head. If he lived to eighty-nine, he'd never understand a woman's prerogative to change her mind at the most inopportune of times.

'Would you mind telling me why?' He fought to maintain a quiet tone.

'Uh . . . ' In her bare feet and flannel

nightgown, she looked as guilty and innocent as a child caught playing dress-up in her mother's bedroom. However, soft curves swelled beneath the flannel. Soft, desirable woman. 'I'm a light sleeper. If I tell myself to wake up at five, I will. I don't need an alarm.'

'But I have an alarm. I just set it.' He tapped his watch.

'What if it malfunctions? What if you hit a button tossing over in your sleep, and the alarm doesn't go off?'

'I'll set my cell alarm for backup.'

'What if both alarms work, but you sleep through all the buzzing and ringing, and the noise wakes the Willoughbys, and they find you dead to the world in the bunk room? Our cover will blow sky-high.'

'You're kidding. *You* won't wake up first and stop them from locating me, light sleeper that you are?'

'So what if I do wake up? You'll be in the room down the hall! Anything could happen, Justin. Any number of complications. I — *we* can't botch this.'

119

He might have resented her accusation that he was alarm-inept if her long list of rationalizations didn't shout loud and clear that something other than his sleeping patterns was at stake. He wouldn't force the issue. He'd roped her into this mess. If she wanted to play Girl Guide by camping out in the bunk room for one night, so be it. He'd sleep there tomorrow night — or he wouldn't sleep at all.

'Fine, you take the bunk room, but you're using the alarm.' He unstrapped his watch and passed it to her. 'I won't take no for an answer.'

Sighing, she slipped on the watch and adjusted the strap. She tugged down her nightgown sleeve to cover the dial.

Justin grabbed a pillow from the bed. 'And this.'

Her nose wrinkled. Now she had a problem with the pillow?

He counted silently to ten. 'Magee, there are sleeping bags in the bunk room, but no pillows. Whoever's using the cabin brings extras if needed. Considering we're supposed to be a couple, I didn't do that. If you'd like a pillow, you'll need to take one from this room or find an old one in the linen closet.'

She chewed her lip. Was the idea of sleeping with his pillow really that disturbing?

She stared at her feet. 'All right,' she whispered. She snatched the pillow and cracked open the door. She stuck out her head, then yanked it back in. 'Coast's clear. I'll see you bright and early.'

'Five a.m.'

Giving a thumbs-up, she tiptoed into the hall. Justin fetched the sleeping bag from the bedroom closet. He spread it on the floor between the wall and the double bed for ease of quick stashing beneath the bed, should the need arise.

He'd promised Magee they wouldn't sleep in the same room. Despite the complications the evening had produced, he'd kept his word. However, he had zero intention of claiming the bed and leaving her the carpet come morning. After several hours of sleeping on a spongy bunk bed mattress, she'd welcome a bit of shut-eye on something firm and warm.

Like him.

He punched the remaining pillow into shape. *Can it, Kane.* While he and Magee might have burned up the beach with their practice kiss last night, she'd made it clear she wasn't interested in a repeat performance.

Good. Neither was he.

Yes, you are.

'No, I'm not,' he grumbled.

This weekend was about business.

Nothing else.

* * *

Magee crept along the shadowy hallway, gripping the blue pillow that might have once cradled Tina Johnston's head. She hadn't wanted to irritate Justin more than she already had by

122

refusing the stupid thing, but she wouldn't sleep on it. No, she had a plan. Step A: exchange the pillow with another from the linen closet. Step B: lock herself in the bunk room until the inhuman hour of five a.m.

She sidled past the master suite and opened the closet door across the hall from the communal bathroom. She scanned the darkened shelves. The closet held enough extra sheets and blankets to warm the entire population of Whistler during the decade's worse blizzard, but where were the pillows?

She craned her neck. Two lumps nestled between a stack of blankets on an upper shelf.

Squeezing the Tina-maybe pillow against her hip, she stretched on tiptoe, grunted, stretched again — and grabbed.

Success! Her fingers clamped the corner of a pillow.

'Tina? Is that you?'

Magee froze. *Oh no. Kate.* Right behind her.

Goosebumps prickling her neck, she released her prize. As the hallway flooded with light, she faced her guest.

'It is you.' Kate grinned. 'Fancy that.' The younger woman wore sexy, frothy baby dolls that made Magee feel even more like a frump in comparison.

Interesting, Kate carted a pillow.

'Kate! I hope I didn't wake — *oof!*' A cascading mass of blankets toppled Magee to the carpet. Dropping the Tina-maybe, she shielded her head with her elbows as a beige wool blanket enshrouded her. The closet pillow whacked her shoulder and thudded to the floor.

Kate gasped. 'Tina, are you hurt?' The younger woman's muffled voice carried through the itchy wool.

Magee coughed and shoved fuzzy fabric out of her face. 'No,' she said as Kate reached her. Humiliated beyond redemption was more like it. What a time for her klutz gene to kick in.

She batted beige wool off her head. 'Just getting a blanket,' she mumbled.

'Well, you've done that, haven't you?' Giggling, Kate placed her pillow on the floor. 'You look a sight. Hold on, give me your hand.'

Kate tugged her upright. A second blanket had woven between Magee's legs. She and Kate danced an awkward box step before the blanket dislodged.

'Thanks.' Cheeks hot, Magee accepted Kate's help tidying the closet.

Kate retrieved the non-Tina pillow. 'I'll store this away.'

'No, not that one. It's mine.'

'Oh?' Kate gazed at the yellow pillowcase. 'I thought you had the blue one.'

'I did, but — ' Magee couldn't very well explain that Justin's ex-girlfriend might have slept on the blue pillow. Not when Magee was supposed to be that girlfriend — and not the 'ex' sort, either. 'It's too new. Too firm. Yes, that's it. It hurts my neck.'

'Too firm?' Kate blinked at the blue pillow lying on the floor. 'Is it foam?'

Magee nodded. 'Not the chipped

kind. The contoured kind.'

'Lovely.' Kate handed over the yellow pillow, retrieved the Tina-maybe, and squeezed it. 'Yes, this will do nicely. Nate's allergic to feathers, you see, and the pillow from our room is some sort of down. Poor soul, he tried being noble, but his eyes are red as a rabbit's already.'

'Really? Kate, I'm sorry. Justin — I mean, we should have thought to ask if you or Nate have allergies.'

'Never mind. It's not so bad, and Nate will like this contoured number.' Kate stuffed the feather pillow into the closet. She handed Magee the folded blanket. 'You'll be needing this, then.'

'Thanks. Heh-heh. Can't forget that. It's why I'm out here, right?' She sounded like a warped copy of a canned sitcom track. Why couldn't she stop with the inane fake laughter?

Kate's gaze flicked to Magee's buttoned-to-the-neck flannel night-gown. 'I wonder if I'm dressed warm enough? Does it get chilly during the night at this elevation?'

'Not necessarily. Not after a sunny day like today.' Magee fumbled with the thick blanket, stacking it on top of the hard-won pillow balanced on her forearms. She pressed her chin into her load. 'Justin likes this nightgown.'

'Ah.' Kate's brown eyes glimmered. 'Aren't you hot?'

'Th-that's the thing. Justin likes me hot.' Perspiration dampened Magee's armpits. *Wonderful.* She felt like she was trapped in a furnace with the thermostat set too high, and now her guest probably thought she and Justin engaged in let's-pretend-I'm-a-nervous-virgin sex games. 'I'd better return before he misses me.' *Go into your bedroom, Kate. Go now.*

As soon as the woman shut the door, Magee would skedaddle to the bunk room.

Kate stepped as far as the light switch. 'You've quite a load. I'll stay put till you're in your room before I turn out the light.'

127

'No, that's okay.'

'I insist.'

So do I.

However, Magee knew she shouldn't protest too much, so she scuttled back to her and Justin's supposed love nest with her nightgown catching at her legs and the blanket scratching her chin.

At the door, she turned. Kate smiled.

'Goodnight,' Magee hinted. *Go into your bedroom, Kate. Go NOW.*

Kate stood there, wiggling her fingers. 'Nighty-night.'

Cheerio. Magee barreled into the darkened bedroom. The door slammed behind her. *Oops.* Dumping the blanket and yellow pillow onto the carpet, she sagged against the door. Her palms prickled with sweat.

A shadow the size of Justin's head popped up in front of the small dresser between the far wall and the bed.

'What are you doing here?' the shadow whispered.

She flipped on the light. 'Why are you on the floor?' she whispered back.

He squinted. 'I'm sleeping.'

She begged to differ. One usually slept on the bed, not the floor beside it.

'*Magee*,' he whispered.

She sighed. 'I ran into Kate in the hallway.'

'What?' Scrambling to his feet, he battled the sleeping bag clinging to his sweats. 'What was she doing?' He pushed the sleeping bag off his hips and strode to the pillow and blanket at Magee's feet.

'Nate's allergic to feathers. Kate had to find him another pillow.'

'Shit.' He rubbed the back of his neck.

'You're telling me. I almost blew it.'

He looked up. 'But you didn't?'

'I don't think so.' She gazed at his enticing pecs, and the temperature in her flannel furnace rocketed a few thousand degrees.

Sidestepping the blanket and pillow, she placed a respectable distance between her itching-to-touch-him fingers and Justin's naked chest and abs.

God, those abs. He sported a veritable six-pack.

'I told Kate I couldn't sleep with a contoured pillow,' she whispered.

'She bought that?'

'I think so.'

'Good.' He eyed the heap of beige wool. 'Why the blanket?'

'Don't ask.'

He bundled the blanket with the pillow and carried them to the bed. 'What happened to your hair?'

'Don't ask that, either.' Magee swiped a hand through her tangled mop.

'Is there anything else I *can* ask?'

'Nothing that pops to mind.'

His jaw firmed. 'Fine.' He held out his hand. 'My watch.'

'What?' She clamped her wrist. 'Why?'

'You had your chance. Now it's my turn. I'm sleeping in the bunk room. Therefore, I need an alarm.'

'*I'm* sleeping in the bunk room,' she whispered.

130

'Not anymore,' he whispered back.

'But Kate could be lurking in the hallway.'

'Yeah, that's likely.' He strode to the door and inched it open. His head popped out a moment. He quietly shut the door again. 'Was the light on when you were with her?' he asked.

Magee's heart pounded. 'Yes,' she squeaked.

'It's out now, so she must be in her room.'

Magee peered at him. Had he asked about the hallway light to trick her? Well, bully for him, if that was how he got his jollies. She'd already accomplished Step A of her plan by getting rid of the blue pillow. She might not have succeeded in her second goal of sealing herself in the bunk room, but that didn't mean she needed to sleep on the bed on which Justin had possibly tumbled around with Tina.

No, she'd sleep on the floor in the sleeping bag he'd thoughtfully spread out.

Suppressing a grin, she handed him the watch. He checked the alarm before fitting the strap to his wrist.

'The pillow,' he whispered, snapping his fingers as if he expected her to skip merrily to the bed and fetch the non-Tina pillow.

'Why not use the one you had?' Now bunched up on the sleeping bag.

He shook his head. 'What does it matter?'

'It's newer?'

'The pillows aren't new, just the mattress.'

'It's contoured. It'll feel better on your neck.'

He closed his eyes briefly. 'The only orthopedic pillow in the place is the one you fobbed off on Kate.'

'I didn't *fob* it off on her. She wanted it.'

'Whatever.' He trudged to the mussed sleeping bag and grabbed the second blue pillow.

'Uh, snap on the lamp while you're there.'

132

He did as she asked. 'See you at five,' he said, sweeping past her. He peeked out the door again, then left the room.

Collecting the blanket and non-Tina pillow, Magee turned off the room light and trundled to Justin's sleeping bag. Crouching, she layered the blanket beneath the bag as padding and killed the lamp. She climbed into the sleeping bag and adjusted her nightgown over her legs.

Her head sank onto the pillow, and she closed her eyes. 'Ahhh.' In thirty seconds, she'd fall asleep.

No such luck.

The warmth of the sleeping bag radiated through her nightgown, and dots of perspiration beaded between her bra cups. Images of Justin occupying the makeshift bed blossomed in her mind.

She unlatched two buttons at her throat, rolled onto her side, and stared into the dark cavern beneath the bed. A trail of sweat trickled down her spine. *Phew!* Whoever said heat rose? A few hours of roasting like this and she'd be as crisp as the skin on her mother's Christmas turkey. Now that Justin had vamoosed, she might have to consider losing the nightgown — or her bra and panties.

Or getting up and cranking open the window.

She unzipped the sleeping bag. The bedroom door creaked.

She stiffened in the bag. On second thought, she'd remain fully dressed.

Sitting up in the darkness, she peeked over the bed. Justin leaned against the closed door, breathing heavily. Strange, she couldn't make out the blue pillow.

She clambered out of the bag and switched on the dresser lamp.

'Why are you back here?' she whispered.

His gaze swung to her. 'Why the hell are you on the floor?'

'Trying to sleep.'

'But *I* took the floor so you wouldn't have — ' His hand chopped the air. 'Forget it.' He crossed the room and sagged onto the bottom of the double bed. 'I ran into Nate in the hallway.'

'What?' Magee groaned.

'He wasn't actually *in* the hallway. I was. He was walking up the stairs in the dark.' Gaze grim, Justin glanced at her. 'Apparently, he went downstairs to get some 'particulars' from the purse Kate left in the foyer, and he didn't want to bother us by turning on lights.'

'Particulars?'

'I assume he meant condoms. I didn't try to see what he was carrying, and I certainly didn't ask.'

'Oh. Right. Good call.' She hesitated. 'What happened to your pillow?'

He rolled his eyes. 'The bathroom door was open, so when I heard Nate on the stairs, I tossed the pillow into the tub. I didn't have time to race into the can after it, so I faked like I was coming out. I could have said I was heading *to* the bathroom, but hearing Nate rattled me.' Justin's hand fisted on his thigh. 'Damn it, Magee, I'm sorry. This bunk room idea won't work.'

Magee slumped beside him on the bed. Her obsession with Tina's months-old presence in the cabin withered beneath the prospect of ruining the weekend with her silliness.

'We probably shouldn't have tried to switch rooms in the first place,' she admitted.

'That's not what I meant. When you agreed to help me, I said we'd pretend to share a room, and that's what we'll do. We just need to wait awhile before trying another switch.'

'I . . . I don't mind if we sleep in the same room, I guess.' She glanced back at the mattress. A vision of her and Justin deliciously naked and tangled together on the sheets swamped her mind. Heart racing, she looked at him. 'Um, yeah, I can put up with sharing the room if we have to.'

His eyes darkened. 'I don't want you to have to 'put up' with anything. But the bunk room door has been known to squeak, and after two near-misses with the Willoughbys we can't chance a

136

third.' He checked his watch. 'Another hour should do it. Nate said he was wiped. I can't imagine he and Kate will be 'busy' in an hour.'

'An hour?' All right, she'd sleep in the damn bed already! Clearly, she had more pressing matters to worry about — like surviving another sixty minutes without surrendering to the madly rushing temptation to jump Justin's bones.

6

'How about this one?' Justin selected a plain brown teapot from the limited assortment on the souvenir shop shelves. 'Surely, you can't object to this one.' He held up the teapot for Magee's inspection. She'd dismissed the last four he'd shown her in this store alone. After two excruciating hours of indulging in her and Kate's shared passion for shopping, his patience rode a frazzled edge.

Magee shrugged. 'I don't understand why you need another teapot. What's wrong with the one at the cabin?' She licked the remaining scoop of her triple-decker ice cream cone, the pink tip of her tongue darting from between shiny lips.

Tearing away his gaze, Justin searched out the Willoughbys. They stood on the other side of the store, browsing a display of Whistler T-shirts. Luckily, the British couple appeared absorbed in the rack, affording Justin a chance to talk to Magee.

He addressed her in a low voice, 'I don't want to argue about this. I realize you're uncomfortable masquerading as Tina, and I'm sorry, but we haven't done the best job of pretending we're a couple so far this morning. Can't you relax for a minute and act like I'm buying you a gift?'

'I *am* relaxed.' Her tongue swirled around another smidgen of strawberry ice cream. 'If you're intent on buying me a present, how about that cappuccino maker a couple of stores back? I'm more of a latte person. Frankly, Justin, I doubt a Brown Betty teapot would impress Kate.' She smiled.

He sucked in a breath. Between the almost sensual attack on her ice cream and her confusing female opinions, she was quite simply driving him nuts. His libido *and* his state of mind.

In hindsight, last night had progressed well enough — if he dismissed the way Magee had scurried to the opposite side of the bedroom whenever he'd approached her. They'd taken advantage of the extra hour to study the cheat sheet and discuss the advertising strategies she'd developed in anticipation of a signed deal with Willoughby Bikes. Justin's subsequent rescue of his pillow from the bathtub and second attempt to sneak into the bunk room had proceeded without a hitch.

He hadn't experienced difficulty with getting up at five, either. His fantasies of Magee minus her granny nightgown had forced him to count the ceiling panels half the night, rendering sleep elusive. He'd returned to the bedroom at dawn to grab a change of clothes only to discover her sleeping on *top* of the bedspread instead of beneath the covers like a normal person. Her curvy body swathed in prim flannel had prompted another flurry of lurid fantasies in his mind.

At least she'd deigned to take the bed and not the down-filled bag on the floor. However, her aversion to using any pillows or linens he might have come into contact with rankled. He might not believe in sleeping around, but neither was he accustomed to a woman shirking from the slightest possibility of sharing a room. In Magee's case, now he had to deal with the added complication of passing himself off as her lover while rarely kissing or touching her.

'The cabin doesn't need a cappuccino maker,' he muttered. 'It does, however, require a new teapot.'

Her lower lip pushed out in an exaggerated piqued-lover pout. 'Then the teapot isn't a gift for me.'

'No, it isn't. But you already knew that.'

Justin averted his gaze as she savored her slowly diminishing ice cream. With the exception of Magee, each member of their group had ordered single or double scoops and then had quickly polished off their cones. However, Justin's co-conspirator had to make *her* three scoops last longer than a box of chewy taffy — arousing and annoying him with her constantly flicking tongue.

He lowered his gaze to the sleeveless yellow top she wore over a bikini the bluish-green shade of the Caribbean Sea. *Wrong detour.* The tanned skin of her upper chest tempted him as much as her ice-cream-glossed mouth.

He tightened his grip on the teapot. 'Now, in your opinion as my girlfriend, will this brown thing do the job for the cabin or not?'

'That depends.' Her chin tilted. All Magee this time — no Tina. 'What job?'

'Stopping hot tea from spilling on Nate.'

Her light green eyes flashed. 'Yeah, that's what I thought,' she half-whispered. Her lover demeanor evaporating completely, she shot a glance to the Willoughbys. 'For your information, that teapot is damn heavy,' she murmured. 'The spout is too big, or malformed, or something.

I did my best with it last night and again this morning.'

'Take it easy,' he whispered, stepping away from the display shelves as a tourist jostled for browsing space near the souvenir spoons. Cupping Magee's elbow, he urged her aside. Her soft skin heated his palm. 'I'm not calling you down,' he whispered. 'Far from it. That chunk of clay at the cabin is my mother's idea of practical art. She won't be too happy to hear how useless it is as a functioning teapot.'

'Then you're *not* implying the near-spillage last night was my fault?'

'Of course not.' Although she hadn't helped matters by filling the pot to the rim. 'I'm only trying to avoid disaster by replacing it before someone gets burned.'

She beamed. 'In that case, buy away.' She slipped the fingers of her free hand into the front pocket of her denim shorts. Her oversized purse bobbing against her hip in time with the two bulging shopping bags she'd acquired during their never-ending shopping expedition, she tossed him a sassy, see-you-later-lover glance and sashayed to the Willoughbys.

Justin remained rooted in place, holding the freaking teapot. Huh? What had that been about? Had he given Magee the impression he blamed her for any of the snafus they'd encountered since their arrival in Whistler?

He shifted his feet, his hiking sandals scuffing the souvenir shop floor. Okay, maybe he'd screwed up last night when he'd chewed her out for complicating their plan to sleep in separate rooms. No wonder she'd jumped to the wrong conclusion. She'd probably misinterpreted his grouchy mood as him believing she couldn't pull off her role.

In reality, his growing attraction to *her* was the problem.

He'd better follow his own advice and take it easy. Stop his mumbling and grumbling and concentrate on his goals. Forget this insane fascination with Magee Sinclair that threatened to mush his brains and instead concentrate on maintaining positive forward momentum toward signing the Willoughby Bikes deal.

Like a chip off the old man's block, he didn't possess the emotional insight to nurture a relationship with a woman right now, anyway. He only had to consider the wreckage of the six months he'd dated Tina to realize that.

All this time, he'd thought he'd known Tina Johnston. However, he hadn't read Tina well enough to understand she wanted far more from life than what she'd *said* she wanted.

Better to stick with his master life plan and refrain from pursuing a woman as captivating as Magee Sinclair until he'd grown his business to the point where he could slow down, change gears, start thinking commitment, and even marriage and family.

One step at a time. Steady and focused. No diversions.

No matter how cute and sexy.

He glanced over to the T-shirt racks,

where Magee stood chatting with the Willoughbys. Something Magee said caused Kate to break out in a wide smile. Nate chuckled in response, and Magee's tinkling laughter floated to Justin's ears.

Stomach sinking, he strode to the cashier to pay for the boring brown teapot.

★   ★   ★

'I'm having a marvelous time! Tina, isn't the shopping brilliant?' Kate gushed to Magee as they stepped out of a trendy clothing store into the tourist-packed Whistler Village Stroll. 'Nate will get a kick out of these Y-fronts I bought him.' Kate tugged a pair of men's briefs out of her bulging shopping bags. She giggled at the cartoon rhinoceros — complete with lecherous grin and a huge purple horn — depicted against gray cotton. 'If he's not too keen on wearing them, I'll give them a go.'

'He'll love them,' Magee said, trying to duplicate Kate's positive energy — and failing. Why did Justin have to suggest that he and Nate discuss business outside the Whistler Starbucks while she and Kate continued shopping, anyway?

Not that Magee minded spending time with Kate. The younger woman's cheerful disposition matched Magee's own usual zest for adventure. Under different conditions, she could easily imagine Magee Sinclair and Kathryn Willoughby as friends.

However, in this particular and most peculiar situation, Magee Sinclair didn't exist. And Magee-a.k.a.-Tina's head spun from the effort of maintaining her ruse without her accomplice hanging around to help her stay on-track.

She glanced at her watch. 'Aren't we meeting the guys for lunch at one? It's ten past. I'll text Justin.' She pretended to rummage in her tote bag for her cell. 'Darn, I forgot my phone at the cabin.'

Buried in a dresser drawer. On purpose. A genius strategy designed to minimize either of the Willoughbys noticing pictures of Monster, Magee's parents and friends, her personal apps, or the phone numbers of her advertising contacts. None matched 'Tina's' family and interests.

Yes, genius. If she said so herself.

'Not to worry,' Kate chirped. 'I'm on holiday. I left my mobile in London. We're free of them! Free, I say.' She returned the underwear to a bag. 'Nate and Justin have plenty to natter about. One more shop, Tina. Please?' Her face scrunched like a pleading little girl's.

Magee adopted a playful, motherly tone. 'All right, just one. But only if you're good. Although I can't imagine what else either of us possibly needs.'

Kate pointed out a tiny store on their right. 'A raincoat?'

Magee glanced at the sign painted in the window: *The Raincoat Rendezvous*. She smiled. While it had rained at some point during the night, the sky had cleared shortly after breakfast. Besides . . .

'Um, Kate, that place doesn't sell raincoats. Raincoat is slang in parts of North America for — '

'I know the slang, Tina.' Kate grinned. 'Nate and I visited the same shop in California. Sorry, did you think I meant a mac?'

'A what?'

'A mac . . . what Nate and I would call a raincoat. You know, for when it's pouring with rain.'

'Uh, yeah, that's what I thought.'

Chuckling, Kate tugged Magee into The Raincoat Rendezvous. Hip-hop music blared from speakers concealed in vinyl-covered, rain-slicker-yellow walls. A clerk who looked barely nineteen, in long blond pigtails, white bibbed shorts, and a pink T-shirt bounced over to greet them.

'Hiya! I'm Dini. Welcome to The Raincoat Rendezvous. How may I help you prepare for *your* special rendez-vous?'

'We'd like to have a look-round at

your latest stock, please,' Kate replied.

'Cool.' Dini popped her gum. 'Hey, I like your accent.'

'Ta. I like yours.'

'Cool.' Crooking a finger, Dini escorted them to merchandise samples displayed on multicolored pegboards hanging on the vinyl walls. A marginally older but no less effusive clerk handled a small lineup of customers at the cash register.

A couple of minutes later, Dini had paraded Kate and Magee around enough varieties of protection to last Magee several years: condom packets fashioned into dangly earrings, condoms tucked into plastic key chains that opened to reveal a hidden compartment, condoms disguised as fortune cookies. At another time, she would have found Dini's excited prattle and product descriptions a hoot. But they were already late to meet the guys. Would Justin be annoyed, worried, or pissed off?

Magee oohed and ahhed along with

Kate over a selection of edible body paints that could prove useful were Magee and Justin actually a couple. Particularly the chocolate . . . and the pineapple. Possibly the cherry. Definitely the coconut. Raspberry, too. It matched her nails.

She rotated the container of raspberry paint in her hands, worrying her lip with her teeth. Damn it, what would Justin want her to do? Hustle Kate along or indulge her? What would *Tina* have done? The cheat sheet didn't cover the discussion and buying of condoms!

'Come on, Tina, look lively,' Kate said from two displays away.

Magee put down the container. 'Sorry!' She hurried over to Kate and Dini.

'I'm wondering what you think of these flavored Johnnies?' Kate showed Magee a gum-wrapper-covered sample condom on the lime-green pegboard.

'Uh.' What would Tina say?

Dini piped up, 'Bubblegum. The latest flavor.' She snapped her gum.

Magee's stomach somersaulted. 'That's not what you're chewing, is it?'

Dini giggled. 'The condoms aren't edible, just flavored. I'm chewing the real thing.' She blew a small bubble.

Kate laughed. 'Tina, you do go on. I shall purchase a box.'

Dini's eyes lit up. Continuing to chatter, she escorted them to the counter. The second clerk stepped aside to greet a fresh influx of customers.

Behind the glass case fronting the counter, Dini asked Kate, 'The bubble-gum only, or an assortment of flavors?'

'An assortment, please,' Kate replied. 'And, let's see . . . ' She examined the glass case. 'Plus a box of Rowdy Romeo condoms. Thank you.'

Dini rang up the sale. She turned her chipper smile to Magee. 'Ma'am, something for you? I noticed the body paints caught your eye.'

'Well . . . ' Magee pretended to consider her options. 'I don't need anything.' Her body-painting fantasies about Justin aside, she hadn't had the desire to even look at a condom since she'd dumped Brent.

'You're stocked up?' Kate asked, patting Magee's arm. 'Why not buy Justin something fun, just for laughs?'

'For sure,' Dini waxed enthusiastic. 'Or try a box of our custom-fitted condoms.' She swept a hand over the display case. 'There's the Snug-A-Bug for your junior-sized man, the ever-popular Rowdy Romeo, and, of course, the Hubba-Hubbas.'

'I see. Hmm.' Gripping the strap of her macramé tote bag, Magee squirmed. Would she make a better impression on Kate — and, through husband and wife osmosis, on Nate — by buying protection she didn't plan on using or by insisting she didn't need any?

A growing line of customers formed behind them. Magee looked at Kate. Kate gazed back at her.

'Ma'am?' Dini chimed.

A guy in line snickered.

'Um, the last type you said.' Whichever that had been. Magee didn't give a

153

rip. She just needed to escape the store, locate Justin, and glare daggers in his handsome face for leaving her to her own resources.

'The Hubba-Hubbas it is.' Dini whipped out a box and plunked it on the counter.

Kate winked. 'Ooh, lucky girl.'

Bold black lettering leapt from the carton: *An extra-generous fit for the extra-generous-sized man. HUBBA-HUBBA.*

Magee's tummy knotted. *Ack!* If Justin saw the box, he'd — what? Laugh? Turn beet-red? Scream at her?

She didn't know him well enough to predict his reaction.

Holding her breath, she unsnapped her lined tote. Justin would never see the condoms. She'd make certain of that.

Turning aside to evade Kate's potential curiosity, Magee rummaged through her wallet for the cold hard cash that wouldn't betray her identity.

After adjusting the heavy shopping

bags gouging the inside of her elbow, she paid for the package. A fortyish blonde peered over her shoulder. Magee's shoulders tensed. *Freaking looky-loo.*

The blonde peered closer, her breath hot on Magee's neck.

'Excuse me.' Magee's skin prickled. Was this how claustrophobics got their start?

'Go on, give her room,' Kate told the woman.

The nitwit hovered.

Retrieving the receipt, Magee dumped her wallet into her tote. '*Excuse me.*' Stepping back, she bumped the woman. Gently. More like a light tap. A nudge at most.

The blonde stumbled against the snickering fellow behind her. Then, as if meeting the resistance of the lineup, the woman bounced back like a mechanical spring toy and plowed into Magee.

Her open tote sailed to the floor. The contents — the wallet, her sunscreen and lip gloss — scattered.

'Sorry!' Why was *she* apologizing?

The twit on stilettos advanced to the counter. 'Two boxes of Hubba-Hubbas,' she ordered.

Dini blinked. 'Mrs. Mueller? You always buy the Hug-A-Bugs.'

'*Two* boxes,' Mrs. Mueller repeated as Magee dropped to her knees to rescue her tote bag.

Kate crouched beside her. 'Tina, you poor thing!' Kate handed over the small paper bag concealing the Hubba-Hubbas.

'Thanks.' Magee stuffed the bag into her tote, then reached for her sunscreen.

'I can't believe how rude some people are,' Kate said. 'Is this yours?' She held up a sheet of paper folded into a tiny square.

The cheat sheet! Sweat popped out on Magee's forehead. *Damnity-damnity-damn!*

Trying not to seem too grabby about it, she plucked the sheet from Kate's grasp, shoved it deep inside her tote, and finished collecting her things. She mumbled another thank-you.

She drew in a breath. That clinched it. The cheat sheet's minutes were numbered. Magee wouldn't risk the Willoughby Bikes deal for Justin's insistence before they'd left the cabin this morning that she keep the folded sheet in her tote at all times. Not now that Kate had seen it.

No way. Magee had as much riding on this weekend as he did.

She'd claim executive privilege and ditch the cheat sheet the first chance she got.

⋆ ⋆ ⋆

'Look, here they come.' Justin motioned his beer mug toward the two women threading through the tourists crowding the outdoor pub's menu board in the hot afternoon sun. 'Finally,' he muttered beneath his breath. Thirty minutes late — with no cell contact. What was Magee thinking?

Plastering on a smile, he pushed back his chair and stood with Nate to greet the shopping-bag-laden pair.

Nate kissed Kate's cheek. 'Good party?' Relieving his wife of several parcels, he stored her bags on the patio bricks beneath the umbrella-topped table.

'Simply brill!' As Kate plopped her last shopping bag beside her chair, her gaze swept the mugs and baskets of chunky fries. 'Having a pint, are you? And chips? Without me?'

'Yes, well, we each had two iced lattes earlier.' Nate patted his stomach. 'A fellow can only handle so much caffeine when he's feeling peckish.'

'In other words, we're starving,' Justin elaborated, accepting two bags from Magee and stuffing them under the table alongside Kate's.

Kate clucked her tongue. 'Poor chaps.' She sat beside her husband. Wrapping her arms around Nate's neck, she kissed him full on the mouth.

Justin and Magee remained standing.

Following Kate's cue, Justin leaned over to kiss 'his' girl. Magee wriggled as his mouth brushed hers. Barely touched it. He tugged in a breath. They really needed to rehash her less-touching rule before 'less' transformed into 'nothing at all' and exposed their charade for what it was.

He placed a hand on her shoulder. 'You're late,' he whispered in her ear.

'I couldn't help it,' she murmured, cheeks pink. 'Kate needed to stop at one last place.'

'Why didn't you text me?'

'We'll discuss that later.' Her chin tipped up.

Message received: less talking *and* less touching.

'I'll get your purse.' He reached for the long strap of the massive bag hanging from her shoulder. Her hand clamped his, her short fingernails scraping his skin.

'No,' she whispered, eyebrows webbing in another silent warning.

'What the — ?' Damn it, the

Willoughbys were watching the show. Munching fries doused with cider vinegar and grinning like two hyenas stalking a clueless herd. Switching on the charm, he teased his fake girlfriend, 'Bought something you don't want me to see, huh?'

Kate giggled. 'She bought something, all right. Something for the weekend.' She winked as if her meaning were clear. Unfortunately for Justin, it wasn't.

'Lemme see.' He dipped a finger into Magee's purse. She slapped his hand. 'Ow! Aw, honey.' His hand stung. Shit, she meant business.

Lips stiff, she sang out, 'Later.'

Kate and Nate exchanged a glance and chuckled.

'Leave her alone, Justin,' Kate said. 'Sorry, I should have stayed mum anyhow. You know how shy Tina is at times.'

Justin stifled a snort. Whatever gave Kate the idea that Magee — uh, 'Tina' was shy?

But he knew when he was beat. Hands raised in a gesture of surrender, he backed up a step. Magee sat and wedged her huge purse between her hip and the far side of her chair. Faking disinterest, Justin joined her.

The conversation resumed as Nate steered the topic to their afternoon plans.

Justin tried to concentrate, tried to remain indifferent to Magee's mysterious shenanigans in his absence.

Yet, throughout lunch, the question burned in his brain . . .

What the hell was in her bag?

★ ★ ★

By four that afternoon, as Justin and his guests settled at Lost Lake for swimming and sunning, he remained no closer to determining the contents of Magee's purse. However, the Willoughbys' interest in CycleMania had grown substantially throughout the day, providing excellent momentum toward his ultimate goal of signing the deal.

After lunch, they'd stored the massive collection of shopping bags in the stock room of the Whistler CycleMania outlet. Justin had introduced Kate and Nate to the manager before touring them around the facilities with Magee. Once or twice, he'd attempted holding her hand to reinforce the Willoughbys' perception of them as a couple. Each time, she'd tugged her twitching hand free.

Her nerves had slackened once the group had decided to go inline skating — probably because Nate had challenged Justin to a race. Pretty tough to hold her hand while graciously trying to lose to Nate. However, now, with the Willoughbys tossing a beach ball in the water while Justin and Magee rested on shore, she'd re-erected her invisible, hands-off barrier.

Lying on his side, Justin propped on one elbow on his beach towel. Magee had reclined on her back, eyes closed and face tilted to the sun. She drew up the leg nearest him and bent it at the knee.

Another barrier — albeit, a sexy one.

Heat coiling within him, he allowed his gaze to drift over the high-cut bikini bottoms hugging her shapely behind . . . then to her flat tummy . . . the erotic indentation of her navel.

Reaching out, he grazed a finger along her sun-warmed shoulder. Eyes shut, she shifted on her towel. Her arm wriggled, leaning into his touch for a second. Justin smiled.

Suddenly, she stiffened. Her eyes flew open, gaze darting to the lake. Her face reddened.

'Checking for the Willoughbys?' he asked. God, she was cute when flustered.

Hell, she was cute all the time. Perky. Smart. Adorable.

'What are you doing?' she asked.

'We need to talk.'

'About what?'

'This.' He brushed his finger along her arm. Like at lunch, he scarcely

163

touched her. Regardless, her skin jumped. He nodded toward the lake, where Kate shrieked with glee as Nate wrestled control of the beach ball. 'Look at them. We're acting like a couple of stick figures compared to those two.' He paused. 'Magee, you're doing a great job as Tina. You get along far better with Kate than Tina would have. But you freeze whenever I come near you. While I realize you might not appreciate unnecessary contact, this less-touching stuff is putting a real damper on my performance as your lover. Pun intended.'

Her mouth curved slightly. Raising onto one elbow in a position mirroring his, she glanced toward the lake again . . . then at the ribbon of sand between their towels . . . then, finally, at him.

The bikini top plumped her breasts between her top arm and towel. His lower body tightened.

'It's nothing personal,' she murmured. 'Well, it *is* personal, but it's not personally against you, if you know what I mean.'

He didn't have the foggiest idea what she meant.

'Magee, you asked me to cut down on the touching, and I have. But I need to touch you sometime, my sweet Tina. If we don't kiss every once in a while, the Willoughbys might think we're fighting and trying to hide it.'

Magee plucked at her towel. 'Kate thinks I'm shy. Doesn't that help?'

He chuckled. 'No. You're only shy when it comes to me or something to do with me. Now, if you were Kate, wouldn't it seem strange that my girlfriend of six months flinches whenever I kiss her?'

★　★　★

Magee chewed her lower lip. What Justin said made sense. As much as she wanted to disguise the fact that her body burned with need each time he touched her, she couldn't risk placing

165

their plan in jeopardy.

She sighed. 'I'll try to do better. I *will* do better.'

'Promise?'

'Yes.' *Give me a break.* 'I just said so.'

'Ah.' His eyebrows hiked. 'Prove it.'

'What is this, grade eight?'

'Show me, Magee,' he said in a low voice. 'Baby, it's time.'

A faint buzzing began between her legs. She wriggled on her towel. 'Another practice kiss? Now? What if the Willoughbys see?'

'Sweetheart, that's the point. They'll think we're in love.'

Magee closed her eyes. *Oh yes. Love.* Justin didn't get it. Didn't realize the source of her turmoil. And thank heaven for that.

Because she could easily fall for this man — his deep voice and dark good looks, the easygoing side he buried beneath a corporate exterior. If she weren't careful . . .

But she *would* be careful.

If only for the charade, she'd offer

him a taste of her body and save her heart for herself.

Moistening her lips, she opened her eyes. He gazed intently at her.

'All right,' she murmured. Moving closer to him on her towel, she pressed her hand on his muscular chest. Lifting her head, she brushed her lips across his. 'How was that?'

His mouth quirked. 'Acceptable, for starters.'

Her heart skipped a beat. 'You had something more in mind?'

'Oh yeah.' His voice lowered. 'A whole lot more.'

Mercy. 'Carry on, then.' She'd intended to sound blasé. Instead, anticipation lightened her tone.

Fake it until you make it. Her motto for the weekend.

But the way Justin looked at her — like he wanted to gobble her up — didn't *feel* fake. It felt like he wanted what she did. What she hadn't dared admit to herself since the weekend began.

To veer onto a scenic route that could destroy everything they were working toward.

That wasn't smart.

This is dumb. Very dumb.

Wrong. Stupid. Asinine.

His gaze fixed on her mouth.

Her breath hitched. 'I said, carry on.'

With an utterance resembling a growl, he slid one arm around the small of her back and pulled her snug against him. His mouth came down on hers, his tongue quickly seeking hers.

She gasped. Hands splaying on his chest, she tested the sexual waters by slowly tangling her tongue with his.

Ohhh. He tasted good. *So* good. Like want and lust and love and . . . *Justin.*

She abandoned herself to the heat of his kiss, curling her arms around his neck and nestling a leg between his thighs. He groaned. Cupping her rear, he molded her against him. Arousal expanded his boardshorts, and his erection pressed her inner thigh.

Her nipples stiffened to aching points

beneath her bikini top. Unless her tactile senses had completely failed her, she'd received indication that Justin would have no trouble filling out the Hubba-Hubbas.

Filling *her*.

Moaning, she snuggled closer. The sound of scampering feet flew past close behind her. Warm sand sprayed her back, and children's laughter crashed around them.

Omigod, they were making out on the beach! A public beach, no less, with families and impressionable kids.

She bolted upright, dragging Justin with her. His gaze traveled from her hot face to her breasts rising and falling beneath her bikini top in rhythm with her rapid breathing.

'Damn it, Magee. I'm sorry.' His gaze darted to the two boys who must have dashed past them now splashing in the water near the Willoughbys.

'Justin, no, *I'm* sorry.' She'd gone at him like she hadn't had sex in months. Which was true, but . . .

He cracked a wolfish grin. 'Don't be. I've just decided you're very good for my ego.'

She laughed. *This* was the Justin she adored. A man who could make light of their public display to help her feel better.

She flicked a glance to his bulge. 'As you are for mine,' she murmured.

He turned to lay half on his stomach on his towel. 'If you'd stop looking at me like that, woman, things will settle down in a minute — or several.'

'I can't wait that long.' Getting up, she dusted sand off her butt. Heading for the lake, she called back, 'I need a cold swim.'

★   ★   ★

Hours later, Magee hopped out of the van's front passenger seat and arrowed for the cabin driveway.

Justin met her at the hood, foiling her escape. The wide smile he'd worn since their afternoon at Lost Lake brightened his handsome face.

'Hey, wait,' he teased. 'We have a hundred bags to unload and you're trying to get away with taking one?'

Behind them, Kate and Nate, loaded with shopping bags, exited the second row.

'Not exactly,' Magee said. Justin's palm grazed her sun-sensitized skin, and sensual tingles shivered through her. She should have applied a second coat of sunscreen at the beach. However, then he might have volunteered to slather the lotion on her. After her comment about needing a cold swim, he'd chased her into the water. A kiss-filled romp had followed, complete with Justin hauling her around over his shoulder like a super-hot barbarian, his hands caressing her butt and waist. Honestly, she'd endured all the touching she could handle without risking a sexual version of spontaneous combustion. It wasn't like they had to worry about Kate and Nate believing they were fighting anymore.

Far from it.

Frankly, Magee needed time to herself to sort through the myriad emotions Justin aroused in her.

She passed a plastic grocery bag from hand to hand. Her tote bag dangled from her shoulder. 'I thought I'd head to the deck, start the barbecue, dust off the table, that sort of thing.' *Pass muster, excuse!* After all, her watch read ten past seven. Twenty minutes ago, when they'd bought the steaks in the Village, Kate had declared herself ravenous. 'Our guests are hungry, sweetie.' He *wasn't* her sweetie, although he definitely was the sweetest kisser she'd had the privilege of testing out. 'If you wouldn't mind taking my packages upstairs, I might find it in my heart to check the temperature of the hot tub for later,' she added with an intentional mix of lover-like innuendo and playful charm.

'Mmm.' His gaze, bluntly sexual and compelling, flickered over her face to

172

linger on her lips. 'You're on.' He plucked the grocery bag out of her grasp. 'I'll take the steaks to the kitchen while I'm at it. Use the path around the left of the cabin. Kate and Nate can help me cart everything in. We'll meet you out back in a few.'

'Sounds like a plan.' Mindful of their audience, Magee kissed him lightly. Lips buzzing from the brief exchange, she left him to explain their arrangements to the Willoughbys. She picked her way along the gravel path. Reaching the cedar deck, she set her tote on the hot tub cover.

She turned toward the barbecue — and nearly jumped out of her skin.

A woman with sleek auburn hair skimming her shoulders reclined in a nearby lounger. Her short white dress exposed long legs crossed at the ankles. Strappy silver sandals adorned her feet, and her perfectly manicured *long* fingernails, polished an electric midnight blue, typed an impatient rhythm on the armrest. A purse the same metallic shade as her manicure rested on the deck beside her.

She looked for all the world as if she owned the place — and wasn't too thrilled with the prospect.

'Uh, hello,' Magee said. 'Can I help you?'

The woman's head swung. Sharply assessing green eyes honed in on Magee's face. The woman smiled.

'Kathryn?' she asked, standing.

Magee's heart clawed her ribs. *Holy crap*. She hadn't spent the last twenty-four-and-counting hours pulling a fast one on the Willoughbys only to be confronted with a roadblock like this!

The woman's question left little doubt as to her identity.

'Um, no. That is — '

The redhead's smile flat-lined. 'This *is* the Kane family cabin, isn't it? I've checked every place on the whole damn cul-de-sac. This must be it.'

'Yes, this is the Kane cabin. I — '

'Then if you're not Kathryn Willoughby, who are you?' The rude cow planted her hands on her curvaceous hips.

Magee lifted her chin. 'Why, I'm Tina. Tina Johnston.' Batting her eyelashes, she flashed a deal-with-it smile.

The woman crossed her arms beneath her D-cups. 'Isn't that interesting? Because, as I'm sure you've figured out by now, *I'm* Tina Johnston.'

7

Justin spotted Tina through the sliding glass door that separated the rustic living room from the sundeck. Not Magee masquerading as Tina, but honest-to-God, in-the-flesh, claws-extended, and looking-ready-to-blow-her-beautiful-top Tina Johnston.

Why the hell was his ex on the deck with Magee? How had Tina found the cabin? He'd prepared a month for this weekend, and she'd never once requested the address. Had she searched online? Why hadn't she called or texted?

And where was her car?

Get it together, Kane!

He spun toward the Willoughbys. They'd followed him into the kitchen, arms burdened with shopping bags.

Justin's palms prickled. Methodically, he stepped to the sink, drawing Kate and Nate's attention to him — and away from the sliding glass door.

'Excuse me a moment.' Voice hard, he turned on warm water and ran it over a dishrag. 'I should take a wet cloth and broom to Ma — Tina.' Damn it. 'I'll bring in the second load of groceries after that. You two can freshen up.' Something his mother would say. He'd yanked the phrase out of air growing so thin that his lungs hurt.

Nate nodded. 'Righto. We'll run our rucksacks and Kate's carrier bags upstairs. Would you like us to take Tina's up, as well?'

'Yes! I mean, thank you.'

Kate and Nate ascended the stairs with the dozen bags from the women's shopping expedition. Justin's breath hissed out. He might have only a few minutes before the Willoughbys came back down. He had to deal with Tina pronto.

He raced to the sliding glass door. Shit, the broom! He couldn't have Kate and Nate returning to realize he'd left behind half his props.

He retrieved the broom. Gripping the wet dishcloth, he scraped open the sliding door.

As he strode onto the deck, Tina's head turned. Her gaze narrowed and spit sparks at him. Magee, standing behind Tina, crossed her arms and arched her eyebrows.

Two beautiful green-eyed women — prepared, by all appearances, to skin him alive.

He didn't require further indication that the pair had made introductions of some sort.

He closed the door.

'Justin.' Tina shot a pointed glance to the dishcloth. 'You've come to clean up your mess, I see.'

He leaned the broom against an outside wall. 'What are you doing here, Tina?' he asked in a low voice. 'And keep it down, if you don't mind. The Willoughbys are right upstairs.' He tossed the rag onto a side table.

She tossed back her hair. 'Who cares?

I've met your cute friend here.' She flicked a hand at Magee. 'Funny, we seem to share the same name. How clever of you, Justin, to find a replacement for me. On such short notice, too, I might add. If I weren't so insulted that you clearly think so little of me, I'd admire your ingenuity.' She inhaled a shaky breath.

Aw, hell. He'd hurt her. Without meaning to. Without realizing he had.

And now, by bringing Magee to Whistler, he'd done it again.

He softened his tone. 'I don't think little of you, Tina. As you well know, until two days ago, I thought we were doing fine.' He knew better now, since getting to know — really know — Magee. His feelings for Tina had been based on not much more than convenience and lust. He couldn't begin to compare the superficiality of their erotic adventures to the front-of-the-roller-coaster sensations he experienced from merely kissing Magee Sinclair.

Tina valued her pride. She would

179

have struggled with the decision to come to Whistler two days following their breakup. To help him with the Willoughbys.

For that, he gave her props.

'We need to talk,' he half-whispered. 'Not now. Later.' They'd discuss the disintegration of their relationship reasonably, without the threat of the Willoughbys' impending arrival.

Tina blinked long lashes. Her lower lip protruded in a way that once encouraged him to think of sex, sex, and more sex.

Sex until his brains blew out.

Hips thrust forward, she prowled toward him like the runway models she loved to watch on reality TV.

Behind Tina, Magee rolled her eyes.

'Justinnnn.' His name rolled from Tina's throat as she strutted. 'You asked why I'm here. Justy-baby, I've had second thoughts about us. You've been under a lot of pressure with your business lately, and I ... might have acted a bit rashly Wednesday by suggesting we take a break.' Her smile dripped saccharine. 'I forgive you for not remembering our six-month anniversary.' Reaching him, she scraped a fingernail along his jaw. 'As I'm sure you're thrilled to hear, I've come to claim what's mine. Justin, I'm taking you back.'

A dry laugh burst from his mouth. He glanced back to the sliding door. Kate and Nate hadn't yet returned.

He rubbed his jaw where Tina had tried to 'claim' him. 'Hey, don't feel you have to do me any favors. You made a valid point on Wednesday. I'm a heel, and you deserve better. Showing up tonight doesn't change that.'

Her sultry seductress act disappeared. 'Oh really? You might feel differently if not for your actress pal.' She glowered at Magee. 'Tell me you're not sleeping with her, Justin. Tell me you're *not*, or I'll scream so loud your precious Willoughbys will come running.'

'Now there's the Tina I know,' he mumbled.

Magee swore. 'Gosh, she's a prize. Solid gold.' Stepping between Justin and his ex, she informed Tina in hushed tones, 'He doesn't need to tell you. I will.' Her index finger wagged in cadence with her words. 'In the first place, we're not sleeping together. Not that it should matter to you if we were. You broke up with him, not the other way around. We didn't even sleep in the same room last night. The Willoughbys just think we did. All right? So relax. Second, I'm no actress. Far from it. I handle CycleMania's advertising. Which means that if you blow this deal with Willoughby Bikes for Justin, you also blow it for me. And, I have to tell you, I really don't want to see that happen.'

Tina flipped her hair over one shoulder. 'Why should I care about that stupid deal? It's caused nothing but trouble between Justin and me. We might be engaged right now if not for that dumb deal.'

'Wh-what?' Justin gaped. Was that

what Tina thought? That he would have agreed with her spur-of-the-moment marriage and baby plans if he weren't focused on expanding CycleMania?

She couldn't be more wrong. He hadn't started dating Tina as a trial run for marriage. She knew that.

Hell, she'd *concurred* with that.

'Tina, you and I — '

Magee's hand swung up, cutting him off. 'Come on, Tina, think about it. If you don't play along and pretend that I'm you — ' Her gaze darted to the cabin. 'If Kate and Nate — who are heading this way as we speak — find out that you're you and I'm not, then Justin could lose the deal. Do you really believe you and he would stand a chance of getting back together after a disaster like that?'

Justin glanced over his shoulder. Magee was right — Kate and Nate approached from the other side of the sliding glass door. His dreams for CycleMania drained through the slats of the cedar sun-deck beneath his feet.

He was sunk. If Tina wanted to blow his cover with Magee, ruining his expansion plans, he had no choice but to suffer the consequences. He wouldn't further humiliate his ex by telling her they didn't stand a chance together, anyway. Not in front of Magee like this.

No matter what Tina chose to do, he had to allow her to salvage her pride.

At the moment, Tina's pride spewed forth in the form of barely checked rage targeting Magee. 'So then *now* what would you have me do? I've spent the last three hours driving up a mountain and searching for this place. I wanted to surprise Justy. I'm not leaving until I speak to him. Alone.'

'I promise you'll get your chance,' Magee said. 'If you play along.'

A vein in Justin's forehead pumped blood. What was Magee planning?

The deck door scraped open. Lowering his eyebrows, he zipped a questioning gaze to her. She bounced the look along to Tina — who ricocheted it back to him.

Hell if he knew!

'Well, hello,' Kate's cheerful voice issued behind them. 'Who do we have here, then?'

Justin's neck hairs bristled. He and Magee moved back to include Kate and Nate in a ragged circle with Tina.

Magee's face whitened. 'K-Kate,' she stammered. 'Kate and — and Nate. Kathryn and Nathryn Willoughby, this is, uh — ' Her eyes ballooned.

'Erk.' Steel bands constricted Justin's voice box.

Tina smirked. 'I'm Tina Jo — '

'Jo!' Magee burst out. 'Jo — Jo — Johannsen!' Her voice raked like sand on glass. 'Tina-Jo Johannsen. Isn't that a riot?' Her teeth clenched in a fake grin. '*I'm* Tina, and this is Tina-Jo. Tina-Jo Johannsen. Heh-heh.'

Huffing out a breath, Tina nodded. 'Right.'

Right? Justin found his voice. 'Right!'

Nate smiled at Tina. 'Charmed.'

'How do you do, Tina-Jo?' Kate

shook Tina's hand. 'Are you friends with Justin and Tina?'

'Wellll?' Glancing at Magee, Tina stretched out the question.

'New friends!' Magee announced. 'This is the first time we've met. Apparently, Tina-Jo rented a nearby cabin from this guy — the owner — in Vancouver. But — but — '

'She forgot the key,' Justin contributed. Magee was amazing, generating a halfway believable story under these pressure-cooker circumstances.

Tina gasped. 'I wouldn't forget a — '

'She brought the *wrong* key with her,' Magee interjected. 'She rented the cabin for the weekend, but the *owner* accidentally gave Tina-Jo the wrong key.'

Kate clucked her tongue. 'How perfectly wretched. Mightn't a spare be hidden in the garden?'

'The garden?' Magee squeaked.

'The back yard,' Nate explained. 'Tucked amongst flowers would work, as well.'

Red splotched Magee's face. 'Tina-Jo searched for a spray — a spare — but couldn't find it.'

'No, I couldn't find it,' Tina confirmed, slipping Justin a glance that read, *You owe me, asshole, and I plan to collect.*

'Hm.' Nate stroked his earlobe. 'Perhaps you could ring the owner? On the blower. You know, the telephone.'

'She tried,' Justin said. He couldn't leave Magee floundering her way through this hide-saving tale. Especially when *he* owned the hide in question. 'She couldn't reach him. It seems he left town yesterday — '

'For Bermuda!' Tina chipped in.

' — and won't return until August.' Justin looked at Tina. Bermuda? In July?

Kate asked, 'Isn't Bermuda frightfully hot in July?'

Magee giggled. A high, unnatural, breaking-glass sound. 'Some people!' She slapped her thigh. 'He's sailing the Bermuda Triangle, if you can imagine.

He's a Bermuda Triangle buff, Tina-Jo told us.'

Nate looked at Tina. 'With your luck, he might never come back!'

Everybody laughed.

'The thing is,' Magee said, 'she . . . Tina-Jo . . . doesn't want to call a locksmith without the owner's permission. He's not responding to her texts. Probably on a flight, or — or his phone needs a charge.' She inhaled. 'Tina-Jo doesn't want to break into the cabin. That wouldn't be right. It's getting kind of late to think about driving back to Vancouver. She's in a bind.'

'Up the creek without a paddle,' Justin added. Where was Magee heading with this yarn? If he took over, would he muddle her story again?

'She's in a pickle,' Kate commented.

'Properly snookered,' Nate agreed.

Magee nodded. 'Which is why Justin and I have invited Tina-Jo to spend the night.'

Three hours later, Magee could have gladly strangled Tina Johnston. She'd pretended to ask 'Tina-Jo' to stay the night as a way to provide Justin's ex-girlfriend with the chance to have that talk she'd said she wanted.

Talk.

In private.

Magee certainly hadn't conceived of the arrangement as a green light for Tina to drape herself over Justin every other second — *in front of* the Willoughbys.

Yet that was how most of the evening had unfolded.

Following the near-disaster of the introductions, Tina had retrieved her purse and accompanied Justin down the road to get her car and suitcase. He'd ensconced her in the bunk room, where she'd 'settled in' while Magee and Kate had prepared a salad and the men had grilled steaks.

'Tina-Jo' reappeared moments before dinner was served. To Tina's credit, she'd played her part well enough during the meal, probably because Justin paid her extra attention as their unexpected guest. After clean-up, the group reassembled on the sun-deck for drinks. Unfortunately, within minutes, 'Tina-Jo's' acting nosedived.

Magee blamed the red wine the woman knocked back like a rusty old car guzzled oil. Or maybe the shiraz provided Tina a convenient excuse.

Now, Magee and Justin sat in lawn chairs while Tina hogged the director's chair she'd wedged between them. The Willoughbys reclined in twin loungers across from Tina, chuckling and commenting while Justin regaled the group with tales of his mountain biking escapades. Only 'Tina-Jo' deemed it necessary to fawn over each sentence, giggling when the story didn't warrant it and thrusting her breasts in Justin's face as she pawed him.

'Justin, that's so funny!' she gushed before he'd finished recounting his latest adventure. Stroking his muscular biceps, she crossed and uncrossed her legs. The movements hitched up her painted-on white dress, exposing her toned upper thighs.

Justin shifted his arm, but Tina's hand remained glued to it. Nate surveyed Tina's behavior from the corner of one eye. A moment later, he slid a raised-eyebrows glance to his wife. Kate, the picture of English propriety for once, drummed a finger-tip on her chin and hastily looked away.

Magee tightened her grip on her glass of pear cider. How she'd love to toss the contents on Tina and watch the Wicked Witch of Whistler melt away. If Tina's obvious efforts to gain Justin's attention stirred the Willoughbys' suspicions about this weekend, she'd — she'd —

Frick, she didn't know *what* she would do, but she could guarantee the outcome wouldn't be pretty.

At the least, she couldn't continue sitting here in faked ignorance while Tina auditioned for a one-woman reality show and the Willoughbys' imaginations ran rampant. If Magee fabricated her own cycling exploits, maybe she'd shift the focus away from Justin and Tina.

She straightened in her lawn chair. 'Last summer in Stanley Park, my friend Susannah and I — '

'Oh, let Justin finish his story,' Tina interrupted. 'We'll have time for yours later.' She wiggled her shoulders, and her breasts bounced.

Justin's nostrils flared. 'In a minute. I need a refill. Anyone else?'

Kate and Nate nodded like bobble-head dolls.

Prying Tina's fingertips off his arm, Justin stood and collected the empty glasses.

'I'll help.' Tina leapt out of her chair. Her dress crept higher on her thighs, revealing a glimpse of white panties. 'Oops!' Tugging down the fabric, she giggled and pranced into the cabin after Justin.

Magee's stomach churned. *That* was the sort of woman Justin usually dated? No wonder he didn't want to marry

Tina. The woman could suck a vampire dry and not feel satisfied.

Magee quaffed a mouthful of cider.

An uncomfortable silence swelled between her and the Willoughbys. Only the intermittent *zzzt-zzzt* of the bug zapper broke the quiet. An amber spotlight on the side of the cabin cast a glow in the darkness, and the tart scent of towering evergreens punctuated the warm night air.

She picked at a dent in her armrest and continued sipping her cider.

Several more moments passed. *Hurry up!* she mentally commanded Justin and Tina.

'Well,' Kate finally murmured. 'Tina . . . it appears Tina-Jo is quite taken with your Justin.'

Cider rushed down the wrong pipe. Magee coughed. 'Oh no! Tina-Jo's friendly. She's trying to help.'

Nate's gaze flicked to his wife. 'I'd say she fancies him.'

'Y-you think?' Heat swarmed Magee's neck.

'Yes,' Kate replied. 'In fact . . . you know, Tina . . . it might do you well to go inside and help them? Four drinks is a lot to carry.'

Four drinks? Between two people?

Kate must think 'Tina' clueless about her 'relationship' with Justin. Otherwise, the younger woman wouldn't have suggested such a transparent excuse.

How could Magee explain that she *shouldn't* go inside because she'd made a deal of sorts to allow the real Tina time to talk to Justin in exchange for not revealing Magee's identity?

On the other hand, 'Tina-Jo' required coaching on the merits of the subtle approach — and Kate had afforded Magee the chance to do something about it.

Widening her eyes, she feigned a belated pickup on the *Danger! Wildcat Present!* warning Kate had issued. 'Ohhh! I believe you're right. Four drinks can be tricky.' Downing her cider, she stood. 'Make that five drinks.'

'There's a girl!' Kate's chuckle trailed Magee into the cabin.

Magee closed the sliding door behind her. In the kitchen, she placed her glass beside the other empties. A bottle of the English-style bitter they'd bought for Nate sat open on the counter, but where were Justin and Tina? They hadn't gone upstairs, had they? Magee could care less if Tina — or even Justin — wanted privacy for their talk, both possessed the minimal sense to realize they should remain in the kitchen. Here, Justin could mix drinks at a snail's pace while keeping an eye on the Willoughbys on the sundeck. Problem solved.

Magee headed for the steps. Justin's deep whisper reached her ears . . . not from upstairs, but from the direction of the main-floor bathroom. Tipping her head, Magee padded down the hall. The sight outside the bathroom door stopped her cold.

Justin's back was to her. His hands angled low on Tina's hips at a position that could be deciphered as holding the witch at bay — or savoring her curves in the skin-tight white dress. Meanwhile, Tina's stance blared her intentions. Her arms curled around Justin's neck, her fingertips sealed to his scalp like suction cups.

Magee remained quiet, ears pricked.

'But Justy,' Tina whispered. 'Those bunk beds feel awful. I tried out the bottom one. It sags.'

'It can't be helped,' Justin replied. 'Where else would you sleep?'

'With you.' Tina pouted.

'Tina, you know that can't happen.'

'Why not?'

'I already told you why.'

Magee blinked. *Can't happen,* her mind echoed dully. Justin had said *can't*. Not, 'I don't want to sleep with you,' but 'I can't.'

Her heart panged, and she shook her head. *Don't be an idiot, Magee.* Brent had been all about playing mind games with her and any other woman he could sucker. From everything she'd witnessed these last few days, Justin might be the same.

She had no claims on Justin Kane. A few passionate kisses, a fake relationship, and business. She couldn't forget that. They'd fabricated their lover cover for the sole purpose of building Justin's bike store chain — and to rescue Sinclair Advertising from the financial quagmire Magee's mistakes had generated.

For all she knew, Justin planned to resume couplehood with an obviously once-more-willing Tina after securing the deal with Willoughby Bikes.

Tina gazed at Justin. As her head tilted, her eyes cut to Magee and her mouth curved. Crushing herself against Justin's chest, she purred, 'But, Justy, I want you. I want you soooo much.'

Barf. Magee cleared her throat. Loudly. 'Ahem.'

Justin glanced over his shoulder. His serious gaze bore into her. Past her anger and defenses. Straight to her heart.

A dizzying sensation vibrated up her spine, and her tummy swooped. *I'm falling in love with him. No, no!*

What had happened to her vow *not* to fall for another man who played games? Justin didn't want her. He might not even want Tina. However, he might be willing to toy with both of them for the chance to expand CycleMania.

His hands dropped off Tina's hips. 'The Willoughbys?' he whispered to Magee.

Pain sliced through her. She was right. She meant nothing to him. After the soul-stirring kisses they'd shared at Lost Lake, his first concern — his only concern that she could tell — was possibly ruining the deal with Nate.

'On the sundeck. Wondering where you two are, and whether you're really getting drinks or playing Hide the Sausage.'

Justin frowned. 'You're exaggerating.'

Tina hands remained tangled in his hair. She aimed a triumphant sneer at Magee.

'I'm not exaggerating in the slightest,'

Magee murmured. 'Kate sent me inside after you. Lucky thing she did. Have either of you considered that she or Nate might have needed a bathroom? They probably would have tried this downstairs one, seen the two of you tangled together, and then this entire masquerade would have been unmasked.'

Justin peeled Tina's hands off his scalp. 'Tina wanted to discuss the sleeping arrangements,' he half-whispered.

Tina's eyes glittered. 'Tina wants to discuss a whole lot more than that!' She glared at Magee. 'You promised I'd get to talk to Justin,' she whispered harshly. 'I've kept my end of the bargain by staying quiet about who I really am. Now it's time for you to ante up. Tina-Jo, indeed. What a ridiculous name.'

Tina had kept her end of the bargain by flirting shamelessly with Justin? Magee wanted to rip out the waffle-head's hair.

She produced a steely smile. 'Between

getting the car and Justin showing you the cabin, you were alone with him for at least twenty minutes. Wasn't that long enough?'

'Apparently not,' Justin muttered.

Tina crossed her arms. 'I need more time. I want a real chance.'

Magee hauled in a breath. 'You'll get it. Later. Given the way you've been hanging onto Justin since dinner, it looks like you two are in here planning a midnight tryst.'

'Maybe we are.' Tina lifted a shoulder.

'Like hell,' Justin mumbled.

Magee couldn't look at him. If she did, she might lose her nerve.

'Whatever,' she said to Tina. 'Tryst if you want. Just don't tryst right now. Unless you're willing to risk losing Justin?'

The witch's eyes narrowed — Magee had struck gold.

She grabbed Justin's hand. A tingle shot up her arm at the contact. Ignoring the traitorous thrill as best she could, she riveted her gaze on Tina. 'He's mine until the Willoughbys return to England. Live with it or lose him.'

Justin chuckled.

Magee saw red. He considered this funny?

Tina snarled. 'You stupid bitch.'

'In fact,' Magee said, 'it would probably work best if you stayed inside for awhile, Tina-Jo. Say, half an hour? That should give Justy-baby and I enough time to manage a little kissy-face and hopefully stop Kate and Nate from fixating on your slutty behavior.'

Tina's eyes snapped. 'Half an hour? What the hell am I supposed to be doing in here all that time?'

'That's simple. Clearly, as we've all witnessed tonight, you're a victim of hormones gone berserk.' Magee tugged Justin toward the sundeck. 'I'll say you have cramps.'

8

Justin rolled over in the sleeping bag and punched the yellow pillow Magee had commandeered the previous evening into a lumpy mass of chipped foam beneath his head. An hour ago, she'd happily grabbed the nearest pillow on 'her' side of the bed — the blue one she'd refused last night.

Women. Would he ever understand them? Or his reaction to Magee?

Especially his reaction to Magee.

He stared up into the moonlight-streaked darkness. The textured carpet bugged his back, and dust bunnies lurked underneath the small dresser, tickling his nostrils. To top it off, his aching erection jutted against his sweatpants. The damn thing wouldn't subside.

Meanwhile, the woman whose proximity had aroused his formerly most favorite appendage to this degree of perpetual excitement slept peacefully — beneath the damn covers this time — in the double bed a shoulder-width to his left.

Magee.

Miss M. Luanne Sinclair.

Even swathed, as she was, in her high-necked flannel nightgown, the woman's presence tormented him like he'd never been tormented before. He wanted Magee so badly, he felt about to explode. However, he also respected her too much to indulge in solo relief like a teenager slobbering over an Internet version of a glossy centerfold.

He pressed the nightglow button on his watch: two a.m. In a few hours, he and 'Tina' were taking the Willoughbys mountain biking. Where would that leave 'Tina-Jo'? Should he ask her to join them?

His gut soured. *Not a good idea*.

Hopefully, he would be spared that decision — and the prospect of further hurting Tina. With luck, he'd wake up to discover his ex-lover had abandoned her renewed interest in him and planned to beat a hasty retreat down the mountain.

The idea wasn't that far a stretch. Tina's behavior had improved markedly after she'd emerged from exile. Had the effects of the shiraz worn off, or had she finally accepted that they *weren't* getting back together? Justin had tried telling her multiple times. However, talking to Tina Johnston about a subject she didn't want to hear was like communicating with cement.

Blowing out a breath, he sat up. The sleeping bag bunched at his hips, his erection straining against his sweats. Elbows on spread knees, he gazed at Magee. She'd fallen asleep on the far side of the bed, but had somehow found her way to his side while he'd catnapped.

Her breath fanned from parted lips, and his chest tightened. God, he loved to watch this woman sleep. In the moonlight, her honey-colored hair shimmered against the blue pillow like a sexy angel's slightly askew halo. Her chest . . . her rounded breasts . . . rose and fell beneath her nightgown as she inhaled, exhaled.

In, out, then in again.

He scrubbed a hand over his face. *Stop thinking about sex!* He had to stop thinking about sex — and the tender emotions that curled from somewhere deep inside him to mock and consume him.

He unzipped the sleeping bag and pushed to his feet, trying — damn it, *trying* — to ignore the throbbing in his saluting sweat-pants. He'd teetered on the precipice of catastrophe since Tina's arrival, at times barely able to string two sentences together without Magee's quick thinking to support him.

And this was how he repaid her? By obsessing?

He needed a shot of whiskey. He'd settle for orange juice.

Not turning on the lights, he shuffled

205

from the bedroom and snuck down-stairs in the inky darkness. Reaching the bottom stair, he stepped on a lumpy blob.

'What the . . . ?' His arms flung out, slashing the air. His foot flew forward as the blob careened off the stairs.

Whump!

He landed on his ass in the foyer. 'Ow,' he whispered.

Standing, he rubbed his glute. On the positive side, his erection had deflated. Nothing like a little bone-jarring pain to spin a guy out of the mood. He should feel grateful.

He flipped on the foyer light and eyed the blob — Magee's huge purse — gutted of a vast majority of its innards. He'd noticed the purse on the hot tub cover earlier. Magee or Kate must have placed the bag on the steps when they'd started making dinner in the chaotic wake of Tina's arrival.

However, if Magee had moved the bag, why hadn't she carted it upstairs? Why leave it dumped unceremoniously on the bottom step? This afternoon in the Village, she hadn't wanted Justin anywhere near her purse.

He stooped to gather the upchucked items. As he returned them to the bag, he picked up a small red box beside a white paper bag. The box's black lettering jumped out in a 3-D effect: *An extra-generous fit for the extra-generous-sized* —

Jerking, he dropped the box. Then, grinning, he nudged it. So, this was the item Magee hadn't wanted him to see.

He retrieved the box. *HUBBA-HUBBA!*

His grin faded.

Had Magee bought the jumbo-sized condoms for a boyfriend? Her sex life was none of his business, but why else would she have bought protection? In Whistler, no less?

He looked down at his sweats. For him?

Nah.

Well . . . a guy could hope.

'Justy?' Tina's voice, husky with

sleep, drifted from around the corner of the living room. Shit! When she'd said goodnight, she'd closed herself in the bunk room.

Heart pounding, he shoved the condoms and paper bag into Magee's purse. An instant later, Tina entered the foyer wearing a plunging dark blue bra and matching lace thong that displayed her sculpted body to perfection. Her gleaming auburn hair cascaded in seductive waves to her creamy shoulders. Spike-heeled sandals adorned long legs that soared into heaven.

She was every man's fantasy.

And she did nothing for him.

Holding the purse, Justin scrambled to his feet. 'Tina.'

'I knew you'd come.' She offered a sexy, hazy smile.

'I couldn't sleep.'

'Neither could I.' She hesitated. 'I sent you several texts.'

'I . . . didn't get them.' Thanks to Magee's advice whispered during a moment alone while cleaning up after dinner, he'd blocked Tina's number and stuffed his cell into a hiking sock under the bed. 'My battery died, and I forgot my charger. Dumb, eh?' He hated himself for the lie.

'Oh.' Tina's long eyelashes fluttered.

He cleared his throat. 'I came downstairs for juice and nearly broke my neck on this thing.' He hoisted Magee's purse.

Tina giggled softly. 'That's a tote bag.' She gazed at him, her cat-green eyes dreamy. 'I'm sorry you got hurt. I found the tote behind a couch cushion. I moved it so I could rest while I waited for you.' She plucked the bag from his fingers and placed it on the floor. 'Justin.' She licked her lips. 'I've been waiting for you.'

His neck hairs stood on end. 'Tina — '

'Shh.' She pressed a finger to his mouth. The lace of her bra scratched his bare chest, and a wisp of cloying perfume lifted from her deep cleavage.

His nostrils twitched. *Possessed*.

Tina's version of bringing out the heavy artillery. She'd applied the musky perfume with an artful touch. So why did images of Magee fill his mind?

At The Dock . . . Magee drowning in pinot gris. Later, as they'd strolled hand in hand at English Bay, his sports jacket had swallowed her frame.

They'd shared their first kiss that night. A practice kiss, but it had literally moved him.

And their kisses at Lost Lake this afternoon had felt real.

Everything felt real.

Only with Magee.

Tina reached behind him and shut off the foyer light. 'I haven't had my chance yet, Justy,' she whined. 'I'd like it now.' Clasping his hand, she tugged him to the couch. A table lamp diffused a soft glow in the darkened living room.

Damn it. Justin sat beside his ex. What had he done to this woman, who obviously thought a dab of perfume and sexy lingerie could change things between them? Had he been so blind to Tina's wants and needs that he'd hurt her worse than he'd realized? Like his father had repeatedly ignored and hurt Justin's mother, his younger brothers, and him?

Tina Johnston didn't plead with a man. She didn't beg. Yet, now, anxiety tightening her eyes and face, she ran her hands up and down the gray sweats covering his thighs. Her fingers massaging, kneading. *Needing*.

Needing something he couldn't give her.

His skin crawled beneath his sweats. He held her hands, stilling them.

She pouted prettily. 'Justy, I've put a lot of thought into what I have to say. Please hear me through. I'm willing to be number two in your life. Justin, I can be number two. Your business comes first. I can live with that. Marriage, babies . . . I want those things, but I can wait for them. For now, I just want you.'

Justin sighed. Long. Drawn out. God,

he was an ass. Exactly like dear old Dad.

He didn't want to hurt Tina again, but he had to. He needed to tell her the truth. She wasn't the right woman for him. She never would be.

In spite of her beauty and incredibly hot body, he didn't want her. And she deserved to be wanted.

No matter that she'd jumped light years ahead of the understanding they'd constructed when they'd started dating, she deserved a man who'd put her first in his life. But he wasn't the man to do it. And she wasn't for him.

The right woman, he suspected, the woman *he* needed, slept upstairs in the double bed. Where he wanted to be.

With Magee. Loving her. Making love with her.

Not down here hurting Tina.

Gently, he moved Tina's hands off his legs. He picked up a crumpled blanket on the couch and arranged it around her bare shoulders, covering her.

He looked her in the eyes. 'I'm glad

you came to Whistler tonight,' he murmured. 'Because you're right. We need to talk.'

★ ★ ★

As the soft cocoon of night pillowed Magee, she reached for Justin. His strength. His heat. His lips, his body, his —

Sleeping bag?

Her eyes flew open. The erotic dream vanished. Before she'd reached the good stuff. *Crud*.

Slippery nylon slid through her fingers, and she gulped. Omigod, she hadn't been dreaming!

Releasing Justin's sleeping bag, she took stock of her precarious position in the moonlit darkness. She rested on her stomach half off the bed, one arm dangling over the edge. She swept her gaze over the green sleeping bag.

Empty.

Her face burned.

Wasn't it bad enough that her body

ached for the man's touch in broad daylight? Now she'd resorted to groping him in the middle of the night — and he wasn't even here.

Except . . . if he wasn't here, where was he?

She peered at the clock on the small dresser: 2:30. *Oh sure.* After hours of lazing within touching distance of him, managing a fair imitation of a dead body in a stage play, she'd finally drifted off, and he'd taken advantage of the situation to — to —

She flinched. Could he — *would he* — have snuck to the bunk room to sleep with Tina?

The jerk.

The bedroom door creaked. Magee scuttled to her side of the bed and yanked the quilt over her chin.

She slit an eye. Justin padded to her dresser. He rearranged items, placing them aside, then set down her tote bag.

Her heart thumped. How had he found the tote?

Unless . . . he *hadn't* sidled to the

bunkroom, but instead had experienced a strange somnambulistic urge to skip downstairs and frisk the couch.

Justin let go of the tote. Immediately, the top sagged open. He reached for the bag again.

Magee held her breath. *Please don't look inside*. If he found the Hubba-Hubbas . . .

He fumbled with the bag, snapping it shut.

She inhaled.

His head tilted. Had he heard her?

As he faced the bed, she clamped shut her eyes, faking a soft and — she hoped! — entirely believable snore.

* * *

Magee flipped over the sizzling hash browns, sprinkled them with seasoned salt and parsley, then lowered the element beneath the hot pan. The crispy potato scent filled the cabin kitchen. *Yum*.

She'd fry the bacon in a second pan,

then spoon the food into covered serving dishes and shove the dishes in the oven to keep warm. When Justin and the Willoughbys returned from their early morning run, she'd scramble eggs and make toast. Kate and Nate would appreciate a hearty breakfast before the group headed out again. To Whistler Village — and the gondolas. Up the mountain, then back down.

Yep, this was it. The test of her mettle. She was going mountain biking.

Her stomach pitched, and she clapped a hand over her racing heart. *Calm down, calm down*. She could do this. She owned a mountain bike, didn't she? With eighteen speeds, fat tires, and plenty of tough-looking tread.

She just wasn't in the habit of barreling her trusty department-store brand down actual mountains. A meandering path through Stanley Park with its breathtaking views of Vancouver and the Pacific Ocean suited her better.

However, she had no choice. She'd committed to the cycling, and now she had to follow through. Not solely for the benefit of her family's advertising agency, but also for Justin.

The heel.

Last night, he'd disappeared after she'd fallen asleep only to return with her mysteriously acquired tote bag. Then, this morning in the bedroom, he'd made like he couldn't even see the damn tote sitting as big as The Raincoat Rendezvous on her dresser. Yet she still wanted to aid and abet him in the achievement of his dastardly plan.

She needed professional help.

Medication.

At the minimum, advice from Susannah.

Unfortunately, aside from the fact that Magee wouldn't dare risk Kate returning early from their run to discover Magee using her 'forgotten' cell phone, Susannah worked Saturdays. And Susannah's handsome cretin of a boss refused to tolerate personal calls during his precious business hours.

In some ways, the man for whom Susannah slaved reminded Magee of Justin. Both were good-looking, goal-driven, ultra-sexy dickheads.

Although, in the sexy department, Justin Kane won the prize.

A smile tugged Magee's mouth. Jerk or not, she liked Justin far too much — hence the weird feeling at Lost Lake yesterday that she was falling for him. A smart girl would ensure she didn't fall too hard. Like, nowhere near the L word. The one that followed with the letters O, V, and E.

Yes, best not to spell it out. Not even in her head.

She located a cutting board and sliced the pack of bacon with a paring knife. While she couldn't help admiring Justin's tenacity and creative streak, the imagination and confidence required in order for him to have dreamt up the fake-girlfriend scheme, the dictionary packed a lot of pages between A for Admiration and L for . . . that other emotion. The one she couldn't trust.

218

Example, she still didn't know if he'd trysted with Tina. Her gut said no. Before he'd left for his run, he hadn't appeared suitably guilty for a man who might have banged his ex-girlfriend after kissing another woman a few hours earlier. He'd appeared quite at ease, as if a weight had been lifted from his shoulders.

Magee wished someone would lift the two-ton rock of uncertainty from *her* shoulders.

She pulled apart bacon strips. The *clackety-clack* of footsteps sounded on the staircase. She glanced over her shoulder. Tina, dressed in white shorts, a white top, and gold sandals, carried her suitcase and purse down the steps.

Magee smiled sweetly. 'Leaving already, Tina-Jo?'

Tina deposited her bags in the foyer. 'You can cut the act . . . Magee, is it? I know Justin took the Willoughbys running.'

Magee blinked. Apparently, Tina also knew her name.

And *she* hadn't let that tidbit slip.

Justin was the only person in the Kane cabin who could have provided that information. Tally one for the suddenly very real possibility that he had been with Tina last night.

Magee tossed the remaining chunk of bacon on the cutting board. She selected a meat cleaver from the utensil holder and tested the blade for sharpness with her thumb.

'Oh, you do?' She forced lightness into her tone. 'Know he took them running, I mean.'

'Of course. He told me he planned to . . . last night.' Tina flicked her tongue back and forth over her teeth. 'You know, during our *chat*.' She imbued the word with sexual innuendo.

A dull ache throbbed in Magee's chest. So, Tina and Justin definitely had been together. That didn't mean they'd done the horizontal hello.

She tried to take solace in the missing details.

'I guess congratulations are in order,'

she said to shut Tina up. 'Looks like you got what you came for.'

'Yeah, looks like maybe I did.'

Maybe? A helium balloon floated inside Magee.

Quickly, Tina glanced away. A full two seconds passed. Her gaze returned to Magee's again. 'You should have seen what I wore for him, hon. Let me assure you, he loved it.'

'Really?' Magee aimed the cleaver at the bacon chunk. *Whack!* The chunk split in half. 'Tina, you don't have to kiss and tell. I didn't think that was your style.'

'Maybe it wasn't, before last night.'

The woman could talk riddles around the Sphinx. Magee traded the cleaver for the parsley shaker. She shook and shook the herb over the hash browns until the potatoes resembled green mold. 'Whatever. I have a long day ahead of me, so if you don't mind . . . ' She pointed toward the front cabin door.

'But I do mind.' Tina sauntered over. 'He was mine,' she muttered. 'Do you hear me? Until you stole him.'

Magee snorted. 'What are you on? Rest assured, Justin didn't sleep with me following his chat with you.' She thumped the parsley shaker on the counter. 'Tina, you made your bed when you broke up with Justin. That might sound clichéd, but it's true. If you truly care for him — ' *in your own malignant way* ' — then grab your stuff and march out that door. Don't ruin this weekend for him. He'll never forgive you for it.'

Tina's mouth popped open. 'It's not too late for me and Justin,' she said, voice reed-thin.

'I never said it was.' Magee stared the woman in the eyes.

'It's not too late,' Tina repeated. Retreating to the foyer, she picked up her suitcase and purse. She opened the door. 'Enjoy yourself with him,' she said as she stalked out. 'Take my advice, and don't put your heart into it. He hurt me, and he'll hurt you, too. Mark my words, he'll hurt you.'

The cabin door clicked shut behind her. Magee blew out a breath. Her head pounded from dealing with the woman. Slapping her hands on the counter, she stared into the green sea of hash browns.

She'd done it now. She'd ruined breakfast. There was nothing to do but toss out the whole lot and start over.

At least Tina was gone.

Yeah, but you still don't know what really happened.

'Shush,' Magee whispered to the voice in her brain.

She didn't need a running commentary to remind her that the two-ton rock of uncertainty pressing on her shoulders had gained a considerable amount of weight.

★   ★   ★

Justin skidded his bike to a stop by the smooth rock portion of the gently descending mountain path where Magee had dismounted. At the next bend, the Willoughbys waited, straddling their bikes. Nate nuzzled Kate's neck, then said something that made her giggle.

'You okay?' Justin asked Magee. Red patches splotched her chalky face, and her fingers practically strangled the rental bike's handlebars.

'Definitely!' She sounded like an overenthusiastic cheerleader. 'This is great! The bike doesn't handle the same as my, uh, GhostRunner.' She named a brand Justin sold in his stores. 'I'll get used to it, though.' She swiped at a tuft of hair sticking out from her bright red bike helmet, knocking her sunglasses awry. She repositioned the dark lenses and offered a gritted-teeth smile.

Justin studied her. 'I don't buy it.'

'You don't?' Her voice squeaked.

He shook his head. She rode like a novice, not a self-professed weekend warrior: forgetting to perch her butt out and away from the bike seat as she bounced along the small rocks on the path; coasting with one pedal up and one down instead of keeping both feet parallel to the ground; constantly stopping and bashing her calves on the pedals as she dismounted. Justin had chosen an easy route for the first ride, to serve as warm-up. The trail didn't provide many technical challenges.

'Something's eating you, sweet-cheeks. And I think I know what it is. Specifically, who. Tina.' As he'd suggested to his ex last night, Tina had vacated the cabin during Justin's run with the Willoughbys early this morning. 'Did she give you grief before she left?'

The lines marring the corners of Magee's mouth softened. Two mountain bikers whizzed past them, yelling and egging each other on. Magee's head turned, and her sunglasses-shielded gaze tracked the young guys.

'Nothing I couldn't handle,' she murmured.

He'd bet. From what he'd witnessed of Magee's capabilities, she could handle damn near any situation. She possessed boundless energy and determination, an upbeat attitude and fantastic team spirit.

Together, they made a great team. Justin didn't only feel that way in regards to business. Magee ignited a spark in him that, before meeting her, he hadn't realized he'd lacked. Then there was the sexual spark zinging between them, too. Hot. Intense. Exciting.

He wanted that spark to burst into flame and grow. He wanted to burn in her fire.

'Well, you don't have to worry about Tina. She's gone, and she's not coming back.'

Magee studied him. 'You sure about that?'

He nodded. 'We talked everything through last night. She knows we're over.'

'She does?' A genuine smile graced Magee's mouth.

'Yep.' Last night in the living room, Justin had made it clear to Tina that he didn't want to be with her anymore. No amount of sexual preening or pleading could change his mind. He hadn't wanted to continue hurting her by admitting that he planned to explore his deepening attraction to Magee. However, Tina wasn't dumb. She'd picked up on the spark between him and Magee on her own.

'She's not happy about the situation,' he concluded. 'But she knows.'

Magee adjusted her sunglasses on her pert nose. 'She won't keep trying to win you back?'

'Does it matter? I'm not playing.'

Magee's smile broadened. Justin grinned back at her like a teenager stuck at the top of a jammed Ferris wheel with the hottest girl in class. Exhilaration whipped through him.

Still straddling his bike, he shifted his weight to his right foot and leaned toward her ... so close that the strawberry scent of her shiny lip gloss carried on the fresh mountain breeze. 'What do you think?'

'About what?' she asked in a teasing tone.

'About the fact that I'm a free man. No ties. No other women. Only you.'

A sigh drifted from her lips. 'That sounds wonderful.'

Tilting up her face, she kissed him. Their bike helmets tapped together. Her mouth pressed closer. Justin flicked out his tongue and tasted. *Mmm*. Not strawberry. Kiwi. A tangy difference that evoked the essence of Magee.

She pulled away, whispering, 'The Willoughbys are waiting.'

'You're right. Let's go.'

'Want to ride ahead of me now?' A funny squeak streaked her voice.

'Why? Are you sore?' Considering how her anxiety over Tina and the Willoughbys had affected her riding, her ass might feel more tender than his had after he'd tripped over her tote bag last night.

Her teeth sunk into her lower lip. 'No.'

'Then why would I sacrifice my

228

prime vantage point for watching your cute butt bobbing up and down?'

'Maybe I want to watch your butt.'

'Not a chance. I have dibs. Besides, if you decide to stop for another kissing break, I want to know about it.'

A pink blush dusting her face, she straddled her bike. She cocked her fingers on the handbrakes. Drawing in a breath, she pushed off.

'Remember to lift your butt off the seat when the path drops,' Justin called after her. 'I want an excellent view.'

She began a bit wobbly. Steadying on the bike, she gained speed and arrowed toward Kate and Nate. The Willoughbys mounted their bikes and resumed their descent.

Justin glanced down to check his pedal position. As he looked up again, Magee flew around the gravel-strewn corner.

'Shi-eeiiiizenhowwwserrrr!' Her warrior scream split the air as she whistled her bike past the Willoughbys without placing either of them in danger.

Laughing, Justin cycled off to catch her.

*　★　*

Magee zipped a fervent wish down through the rutted earth to the molten core of the planet that the devil had reserved a cozy spot in hell for her.

Because she was going to die.

Mud splattered from the knobby front tire of her mountain bike, speckling her skin and sunglasses. Her burning fingers clamped the hand brakes, palms sweating. Her thigh and calf muscles throbbed from the effort of maintaining horizontal bike pedals on the grubby track through the trees Nate had requested for their second ride.

And her ass ached from bumping the bike seat far too many times.

Idiot! Whatever had compelled her to lie to Justin about her abysmal lack of mountain biking skills? Somehow saving her father's advertising agency from financial ruin by doing something *so incredibly stupid* didn't seem the best course of action now that she was staring mortality in the face.

She'd barely survived the first ride — that horror show Justin called a 'warm-up.' When she thought about how she'd narrowly missed slamming into Kate and Nate after her perspiring fingers had slipped off the handbrakes, she wanted to crawl down the mountain to the relative safety of the city and hide.

But she couldn't crawl anywhere. No, she had to get through this. She had to pummel her fear into a hard ball in the pit of her stomach, shrug off the pressure of the Willoughbys' good-natured heckling as they'd raced ahead of her on the widest point of the trail, ignore Justin's breathing as his bike followed hers. Ignore everything except the need to prove that she wouldn't screw up.

'Here it comes!' Justin shouted. 'Get ready!'

It? Her throat squeezed. What 'it'?

A glob of mud spewed from the widening track, smearing her sunglasses like a thick trail of slug slime. Her vision obscured.

Adrenaline spiking, she swiped a hand at the lenses.

'Jump the root, Tina! Jump the root!' Kate yelled from a tree-shaded clearing up ahead.

Ba-doomp!

Magee shrieked as her front tire hit the exposed tree root. The impact jolted her head over handlebars off the bike. She tumbled through the air in a bizarre Dr. Seuss-like blur of upside down Willoughbys, inverted evergreens, and acres and acres of —

Chocolate fudge?

9

'Magee — my God!' Justin leapt off his bike. 'Tina!'

Flinging aside the bike, he tore through the ankle-deep patch of mud. Magee lay sprawled on her back, her arms and legs splayed in the sticky muck.

Damn it, he'd blurted her name. He didn't care. He needed to reach her. Now!

In the next second, he sank to his knees in the mud beside her. She lifted her head. Her red helmet perched crookedly on her matted hair. Her sunglasses — bent and dripping grime — dangled from one ear. She pushed onto her elbows, and her sunglasses dropped into the mud with a splat.

Her propping abilities were a good sign. Regardless, Justin gathered her into a loose embrace and checked for broken bones. Running his hands up and down her legs encased in snug bike shorts. Her arms and ribs through the grubby T-shirt. Shoulders and collarbone. Neck and spine.

Her head wobbled on his arm. 'Lucifer?' She blinked at him through mud-splattered lashes.

'Ma — Tina!' This wasn't a time for jokes!

She swiped at the mud peppering her face. 'I'm kidding. Ouch! Oooh. Now *that* feels good.' She smiled as he skimmed his hand along her thigh.

Thank God. The vice grip clutching his chest loosened. Magee couldn't be too badly injured if she could tease him after her tumble into the mud hole which the annual summer rains had created. The high canopy of evergreens preserved the mud patches on these technically challenging bike paths. Despite that Magee had claimed expertise with mountain biking trails in the Vancouver area, today marked her first Whistler experience. He should have ensured she'd heard his warnings about the exposed tree root and potential mud hole instead of allowing the rhythmic bouncing of her curvy ass on the bike seat to hypnotize him into sensual complacency.

At least she *was* experienced, although possibly not to the degree he'd assumed. The lead-up to a wipeout of this magnitude would have terrified a panicking novice.

He ripped off his small daypack, retrieved a tiny flashlight, and tested the dilation of her pupils. They were fine. The breath trickled from his mouth.

'Any dizziness?' he asked. 'Headache?'

She shook her head. 'I'll survive.'

'Let me be the judge of that.'

She gave a puzzled look. 'What?'

He smiled. 'Let me help.' Her brain wasn't firing on all cylinders yet.

Sliding an arm around her waist, he hefted her upright. Once he was convinced she could stand, he gingerly took her bike helmet off her head and tossed it to Kate.

'There's nothing broken, I hope?' Kate asked.

'No,' Justin and Magee replied in unison.

Nate, standing beside his wife on the dry portion of trail where Magee and her bike should have landed, held out a water bottle. Justin returned the flashlight to his pack, then caught the bottle as Nate tossed it.

Justin twisted off the cap. 'Like the lady said, she'll survive.'

Kate punched the air. 'Brilliant!'

Justin firmed his lips. Apparently, neither Kate nor Nate had heard him call 'Tina' another name. If they had, they'd dismissed his mistake as garbled mumbling. Either that or they'd been too occupied cleaning up to notice. All four filthy bikes now leaned against two tall spruces behind Nate. While Justin had checked Magee's bones, one or both of the Willoughbys must have dragged the rentals free of the muck.

Justin had escaped discovery twice in

the last twenty-four hours. First, during Tina's surprise arrival last night, and now today as a result of Magee's accident. He couldn't expect his luck to continue. From this point forward, the lover ruse needed to proceed without *any more* glitches.

'Close your eyes,' he instructed Magee. As he squirted water on her hair, she squealed. Kate passed him a small towel from her pack, and he wiped the mud speckles off Magee's face. 'How's that?'

Slowly, she lifted first one eyelid, then the other. She blinked in rapid succession. 'I can see! I can see!' she said as if he'd performed a miracle. Wincing, she turned to examine the back of one thigh. 'My leg's a little tender.'

'No kidding. Nice road rash, sweet-cheeks.' Justin sprayed cool water over the large scrape. 'It's not bleeding, but you'll feel uncomfortable for a few hours.' He passed the water bottle and towel to Nate.

'No problem. I can tough it out.'

Magee extracted her bent sunglasses from the mud and trudged toward the bikes.

'You won't have to tough it out for long, Rambette. This trail meets the first one around the next corner. From there, it's not far back to the store.'

'You mean CycleMania?' Magee retrieved her bike helmet from Kate and strapped it on. 'What about the gondolas? We have the bikes until four. The plan was to fit in a third ride before lunch.'

Justin chuckled. 'Not today.'

Magee frowned. 'Why not?'

'Come on, Tina,' Kate said. 'You're soaked through. I'd say you've had a bellyful.'

'You're beaten,' Nate agreed. 'What's more, you really should have a wash.'

Magee glanced at her grime-covered body. 'But mountain bikers love mud.'

'Yeah, but you look like you've been swimming in the stuff,' Justin said. 'When we hit the sun, that mud will start to dry. On you. On the bikes.

You'll look like a mud-caked river rat. Worse, you'll feel like one. Itching. Crusting and flaking. Ugh.' They lived on the 'Wet Coast.' Being a mountain biker, she must have dealt with rain and muck before now.

Her determination was cute. Totally unnecessary, but a turn-on.

'I have to keep going.' Her eyes widened.

'No, you don't,' Justin said calmly.

'Yes, I do!'

'No,' he repeated. 'You don't.'

'Yes!' Her voice rose and broke. 'I do!'

'Why?' He stepped onto the dry earth beside her. The Willoughbys ambled toward their bikes, affording Justin and Magee welcome privacy. He curled an arm around her mud-slippery shoulders. 'You came, you fell, you've been conquered. There's no shame in that, baby.' He squeezed her. 'None at all.'

Her gaze flicked over his face. 'There's not?'

He chuckled. 'Nope.' He dropped a

kiss to her lips ... her full, lush, enticing mouth. *Ah, Magee.*

Her cheeks bloomed a lovely rose. 'What about the Willoughbys? We promised them a full day of biking. It's not fair to make them stop.'

'Good point.' Knowing Kate and Nate, they'd agree to shorten their one mountain biking day at Whistler — whether they wanted to or not — unless Justin insisted otherwise.

Well, he'd just have to insist.

'I have an idea.' He waved them over. 'Who wants to hear it?'

★   ★   ★

Magee stood beneath the hot shower spray while the thrumming water rinsed the last globs of mud from her body, her upturned face, and her twice-shampooed hair. Her bones practically groaned with relief as her stiff muscles drank in the seductive heat from the massaging showerhead.

Her tumble into the mud an hour

ago had taken its toll on her aching body. Thankfully, Justin had insisted they both quit riding for the day. No way could she have maintained the incessant pace Kate and Nate had set during the so-called warm-up ride this morning.

Magee would have died trying, though. Until Justin's softly spoken words had liquefied her knees and her resolve, she'd been determined to slog on — as if continuing to torture herself on Whistler's mountain biking trails could erase the lie that had won her the CycleMania account four months ago.

Stopping the flow of the water with a twist of the shower lever, she stepped out of the tub and reached for an oversized bath towel. She fluffed her hair, then shifted her attention to her throbbing arms, thighs, butt, and calf muscles. How did Kate and Nate do it? Where did the British couple get their athletic stamina and ability? From magic vitamins Magee didn't know about?

She couldn't believe that Nate had asked Justin if he and Kate could keep their bikes until Sunday, so they could cycle back to the cabin after they'd had their fill of flying down the mountain. While the arrangement saved Justin and Magee from returning with the van later this afternoon to pick up the Willoughbys, Magee felt like an easily drained, no-name battery next to that pair of English-accented Energizer bunnies.

If she didn't like Kate and Nate so much, she'd feel tempted to throttle them.

If she wasn't so worried she'd lose Justin's business, she'd love nothing more than to tell him the truth.

She dried a foot and propped her heel on the lowered toilet lid. With gentle movements, she rubbed the towel over her lower leg. She dragged in a breath. Her fall had zippy to do with Justin not providing enough advance warning about the possible mud hole, like his apologies in the van had indicated. Magee couldn't mountain bike to save her life. As such, she never should have agreed to masquerade as Tina.

A knock sounded at the door. Magee stilled her towel-covered hands on her ankle.

'Magee? Are you decent?' Justin's voice filtered through the white-painted wood, his tone low, a little husky.

And very, very inviting.

'Uh.' She glanced at her muddy clothes in the corner, then at her naked body. Other than the now-soggy towel, she didn't have a stitch to throw on. Rather than dripping mud onto the carpeted upstairs hall — it was bad enough she'd dribbled grime on the steps — she'd figured she'd have time to shower and run into the bedroom for fresh clothes before Justin finished showering in the downstairs bathroom.

Obviously, she'd been wrong.

Gee, that's rough.

'Stifle it,' Magee whispered to her annoying inner voice.

'Huh?' Justin asked through the door. 'Magee, can you hear me? Are you dressed?'

Her face heated. On top of everything else, now he'd caught her talking to herself.

'Not exactly,' she answered. 'Why?'

'I have something to give you,' he murmured. At least, it *sounded* like a suggestive murmur. Maybe the sexy inflection was a mutation of Justin's voice carrying through the dense wood of the door.

'You do?' She wet her lips. 'What is it?'

'Open up and you'll see.'

This time, she wasn't mistaken. He'd murmured. Oh yeah, he'd murmured, all right. Otherwise, her body wouldn't be humming like a just-twanged mouth harp, her nipples peaking *not* from a chill in the air. Humid warmth filled the small bathroom.

Her heart pounded. Fake it until you make it — her mantra for the weekend — suddenly blared with new meaning.

With Justin, she doubted she'd need to fake a single response.

Well, okay. If he wanted to 'give' her 'something,' she'd gladly take it. All the way.

'One minute!' She finished toweling off, then dumped her muddy clothes and runners in the bathtub for soaking later. Checking her rosy-cheeked reflection in the mirror, she rinsed newly acquired mud splotches off her hands and fluffed her damp hair. A swish of minty mouthwash later, she wrapped the oversized towel around her naked body and secured the layers between her breasts with one hand.

Sucking in a breath, she opened the door.

Justin stood in the hall sporting nothing but a pair of clean khaki shorts, a sex-god smile, and holding a bottle of . . . antiseptic.

Her chest sagged. 'That's what you want to give me?' He presented a small blue kitchen bowl in his other hand.

His gaze drifted over her body

bundled in the towel. 'Of course.' He grinned. 'For your scrape.' He stepped closer. 'The cotton balls are in this bathroom. You can apply the antiseptic yourself or — ' his eyebrows hiked ' — I can do it for you.'

The man did not disappoint!

Smiling, she leaned against the doorjamb. 'Oh really? You'd humble yourself by applying that gunk for me?'

He nodded. 'Your personal physician, at your service.'

Magee chuckled.

'Your attending. Or whatever they call it. Like the character George Clooney played on *ER*.' Justin's mouth quirked. 'My mother has fifteen years of the series on DVD.'

'Mine, too.' Magee's mom glommed all things George. 'I believe Dr. Ross was a pediatrician.'

'Ah.' Justin's voice dipped, his gaze taking the scenic route. 'That works. Because I fully intend to baby you.'

Magee's pulse skittered. If Justin wanted to play doctor, she'd indulge him. 'Okay.' She tightened her grip on the knotted towel. 'Where should we, uh, do it?'

'Seeing as I *think* we're still talking first aid, how about right here?'

First things first, she supposed.

She perched on the lowered toilet lid and arranged the towel over her crossed legs. As she clasped the tucked layers against her chest, Justin moved to the sink and poured warm water into the bowl. He added antiseptic, and a metallic odor billowed from the bowl.

'I'm going to stink after this,' Magee warned him.

'You've smelled worse. Heavy perfume and white wine pops to mind.'

She smiled. He'd referred to their disastrous practice date. Her near-drowning in Possessed and pinot gris.

Her tummy swooped. She hadn't thought men remembered little details. Certainly, Brent hadn't. However, Justin did.

So what if an amnesiac would recall a date from hell like theirs? It remained *their* first date. Their beginning.

Justin collected the cotton balls from a vanity drawer. Bending on one knee in front of her, he placed the bowl on the floor. His gaze drifted to Magee's crossed legs . . . and stayed there.

Her heart raced.

'Part for me,' he murmured.

Vibrations rushed between her legs. 'Excuse me?'

'The towel,' he whispered, voice tight. 'Part . . . the towel. So I can see the scrape.'

Finger-combing her hair behind one ear, she slowly extended her left leg until her toes skimmed his six-pack. The towel slipped open, revealing her upper thigh.

'Very nice.' He cleared his throat. 'However, it occurred to me, this sitting down won't work. You scraped the back of your leg. I need you to stand . . . or lean over . . . or lie down.'

His gaze lifted, catching hers. The intensity in his eyes pulled her into their swirling blue depths.

Where she swam willingly.

Gladly.

Completely submerged.

Her skin burned. 'I vote for the lying down,' she murmured.

She didn't waver or look away. She knew exactly where this moment would lead. She wanted him, and he wanted her. Nothing could be more simple or complicated.

However, right now she didn't want to consider the complications. She didn't want to think at all.

She only wanted to feel.

'Let's go to the bedroom,' she said, allowing him no margin for misinterpretation. 'The bowl stays here.'

His eyes gleamed. 'We'll continue the first aid later.'

He scooped her into his arms. As the towel bunched between them, he carried her into the bedroom they'd never truly shared until now.

Gazes locked, he placed her gently on the bed. Levering himself over her, his face close and the passion shading his features stealing her breath, he slid his gaze over her towel-covered body.

A playful glint entered his eyes. Grasping her hands, he lifted them above her head and pinned them against the quilt.

The towel gaped, exposing her from her tingling breasts to the whorls of heat burrowing between her thighs.

His gaze raked her. 'My love slave,' he murmured, grip tightening on her wrists. 'I have you completely under my control.'

As if to prove he meant business, he coaxed her arms apart. The tiny movements caused the towel to fall away entirely, leaving her naked as Eve and enjoying every moment of the sensual torment.

'Oh yeah?' Pushing up her body, she flipped him onto his back in a fluid motion he admittedly didn't fight.

Smiling, she straddled him — and pinned *his* arms above his head.

Beneath his khaki shorts, the thick ridge of his erection pressed into her bare flesh. The coupling of her moist skin and springy curls against the crisp cotton of his shorts spiraled hot ribbons of pleasure through her.

'Now who's in control?' Lowering her mouth, she brushed a kiss across his lips.

'You are.' He groaned. Dodging a second kiss, he ducked his head and pulled the tip of one breast into his mouth.

Rippling sensations tugged from her nipple to between her legs, and she gasped. His tongue flicked, teeth nipping the hard bud. Magee's grip slackened on his wrists.

'Am I still in control?' she asked.

His hips rocked beneath hers. 'Uh huh,' he mumbled around her nipple.

'You could have fooled me,' she said as he relinquished her breast.

He kissed her deeply.

They rolled toward the center of the bed, kicking off the mussed towel. Their mouths fused, tongues mating and thrusting. Somehow Justin wound up on top of her again. She fumbled with the button of his shorts, carefully lowered the zipper, and shoved the garment down his muscular rear along with his boxer-briefs.

He tossed aside his clothes, and she stroked his silky-smooth erection while they kissed. A moan issued from deep within his throat. His thickness seared her palms, and her pulse raced.

Until Justin, she hadn't really understood the concept of 'extra-generous-sized.' Could she do it? Would she fit him?

Yearning filled her. She wanted them to fit together perfectly. Not only in bed, but in their hearts and in their lives.

'Justin, do you have anything?'

He groaned. 'No, damn it.' His dark head sank onto her shoulder. He lifted it again. 'But you do.' His eyebrows wiggled. 'Hubba-hubba.'

Her cheeks flamed. 'You know about the condoms?'

'I know all your secrets.'

No, you don't.

Magee pushed away the unwelcome reminder. It wouldn't do to get all noble and confess her . . . well, her confession now. She needed time to decide how and when to tell him.

Judging from the haste Justin displayed jumping off the bed and retrieving the condoms from her tote bag, he wasn't in the mood to act priest to her repentant sinner, anyway.

'I tripped on your purse on the steps last night. Some stuff spilled out, including these.' He ripped into the box of Hubba-Hubbas.

'My tote bag was on the steps?' Magee held up a hand. 'Never mind.' She couldn't bother solving that particular mystery right now. Thanks to Kate dragging her into The Raincoat Rendezvous yesterday, she and Justin were ready to rock and roll.

Rolling onto her stomach, she propped her chin on a hand and drank in the sight of Justin's magnificent body as he struggled with the stubborn box. Her heart swelled.

'Need help?' she asked.

'Ah, no. Got it.' Grinning, he held up a condom packet. 'It's okay if I use these?' He tore open the packet with his teeth.

Magee stared at his prominent erection. 'Yes.'

He cocked a sexy half-smile. 'I thought you bought them for someone else.'

'Nope. I hate sharing. I'm a one-guy type of girl.'

'Sweetcheeks, you don't know how happy I am to hear you say that.'

'I can *see* how happy you are.'

Striding to the bed, he flipped her the open packet. 'Care to do the honors?'

'My pleasure.'

He sat beside her on the quilt, and she sheathed him. Slowly. Gently. Caressing his hard length with her fingers as she unrolled the protection.

Passion and desire swept through her. Need and want — and something else.

Something dazzling and brilliant.
Simply soul-shattering and wonderful.

I love you.

Magee kissed him, welcoming the raw silk of his lips on hers.

I love you. The words shimmered in her heart, blossoming in her body. Filling her.

And then he was filling her, too.

Inch by beautiful inch, he pushed into her. Magee's bones melted as her lower body slickened to accommodate his size. She moaned, pleasure coursing through her.

Justin paused before fully entering her. He brushed a tendril of hair off her face and smiled into her eyes.

'I don't want to hurt you,' he whispered.

'You won't, Justin. Please.'

He cupped her face, his thumb caressing her lower lip. Never once releasing her gaze, he withdrew. Then slowly glided back in.

Deeper this time. Then deeper still.

His thrusts quickening. Moving her with him. Moving them together. As one.

Magee kissed him everywhere she could reach. His lips, his face. His chest right over his heart.

Their mouths melded, and her climax spiraled. Gasping, she shattered. Wave upon wave rushing through her until she tightened around him.

He swallowed her cry with a kiss. 'Oh God,' he whispered hoarsely. 'Magee.'

With a final thrust, he pulsed into her, and her world exploded again.

Her soul flew apart and sprinkled back to earth, the joy washing over her as cleansing as summer rain.

Her eyes moistened with sweet tears as he held her. *You've really done it this time, Magee.* And there was no turning back. No quick fixes. No changing her mind.

For how could she change what had settled in her heart?

She'd fallen completely in love with Justin.

Nothing in her life would ever be the same.

★ ★ ★

Justin took off the sweats he'd worn downstairs to start the morning coffee. Pale rays of sunlight streamed through the open bedroom window, and trilling birdsong carried on the cedar-scented breeze. He slipped beneath the cool bed sheets and spooned Magee. As she wiggled her warm rear against his pelvis, a dreamy moan lifted from her mouth.

Curling his arms around her, Justin kissed the light smattering of freckles he'd noticed on her shoulder yesterday afternoon when they'd made love a second time during the Willoughbys' absence. In the middle of the night, they'd made love yet again while soft lamp light washed their bodies. He'd paid special attention to each new freckle discovery, licking and sucking Magee's satiny skin until she'd trembled beneath him.

Now, sexual urgency pulsed in his veins anew. At the same time, his heart expanded and contracted with a strangely welcome emotion that reminded him of melting caramels left too long in the sun. Was this powerful pull deep within his chest love?

He cuddled Magee closer. She released another moan and rolled over in his arms. Eyes half-closed, she kissed him

'Mmm, Dr. Justin,' she whispered. 'Where have you been? This gurney's way too big without you.'

Justin chuckled. He'd left Trauma Room One for all of twenty minutes. 'I ran into Kate and Nate downstairs. Nate wanted to discuss a couple of issues regarding the deal.'

Magee's body tensed slightly, her light green eyes clouding. Yesterday, whenever Justin and Nate had started talking business, she'd reacted in much the same fashion — over dinner after the Willoughbys had returned from mountain biking, and then later, during the group soak in the hot tub before bed.

The masquerade must be eating her up. Magee was a far better person than he was — after all, she hadn't conceived of the ruse — and the continued pretense had beaten his conscience black and blue.

He ran his hands over her bare behind and firm thighs, avoiding the scrape he'd eventually 'treated' in the shower. 'You okay?'

She gave an unconvincing nod. 'What time is it?' Her voice sounded small.

'Five past seven. The Willoughbys went hiking in Garibaldi Park. They'll return around ten. Kate invited us along, but I said you were worn out from your fall and wanted to sleep in. Nate said if you're still in bed when they return, I can knock you up then.'

The corners of Magee's mouth twitched. 'He really said that?'

'Don't worry, he hasn't been poking holes in the condoms. I know, because

I checked.' Justin grinned. He hadn't checked. Although, with another woman, he probably would have. That he didn't experience the same qualms around Magee amazed him. He'd always vowed he wouldn't consider settling down and raising a family until he'd achieved his business goals. However, judging by the stirrings in his lower body, the vision of Magee pregnant with his child *excited* him.

And made him want forever right now. Not next month, or next year. And certainly not in the distant five years his rigid master life plan prescribed.

Cupping her bottom, he fit her snugly against his growing erection. 'Translating, I think he meant I could knock on the door and *wake* you up.'

'Aw. Here I was looking forward to morning sickness . . . with the right doctor to attend me.'

'How about a bit of morning loving instead?' The need to bury himself deep within her drove through him. 'Then I'll make you breakfast in bed.' He kissed her. 'How does that sound?'

Her eyes closed. 'Absolutely wonderful,' she murmured. 'But Justin, I can't keep doing this. I can't make love with you while I'm lying through my teeth.' Opening her eyes, she shook her head. 'Not anymore.'

10

Breath hitching, Magee scanned Justin's face. She'd just admitted she'd been lying to him, yet his gaze reflected understanding, compassion, and even remorse.

Beneath the rumpled sheets, his hands massaged her naked butt. 'Aw, sweetcheeks, I know how you feel. The pretense is getting to me, too. The Willoughbys are flying to England in a few days. Then we can relax.' One hand glided up to caress her breast. He dropped ticklish kisses onto the sensitive hollow behind her ear. 'We can continue our plans for this morning.' He winked. 'When Kate and Nate get back, we'll eat lunch and pack. Then, if you'd like, we can fit in another ride on the mountain bikes before returning to Vancouver.' His hand molded her breast, his erection prodding her thigh.

'Have I convinced you?'

Desire swirled in her belly. The sensual heat in Justin's eyes promised passion . . . and so much more.

It would be so easy to give in to him, to pretend they both meant the same lie. However, months had passed since she'd landed his account, and her guilt mushroomed with each passing hour. She couldn't keep hiding the truth from him now that she'd tumbled head over handlebars in love. She had to confess — and pray he understood.

'No, you haven't convinced me,' she whispered, clasping his wrist. 'Justin, please stop.'

His hands stilled. 'What's wrong? Your scrape? Your head? Are you dizzy?'

'No, it's . . . none of those. I can't go mountain biking again. Not today. Not ever.'

His forehead creased. 'Why not?'

'Because . . . I *can't.*' *Tell him, Magee.* As quickly as possible. 'I own a mountain bike of sorts, but a greenhorn's version of a mountain bike, not a GhostRunner like I said. Until yesterday, I'd never done any actual mountain biking in my life. It's not my hobby or my passion. I just said it was so I could land your account.'

Surprise. Disbelief. Sharp hurt. Anger. All registered in rapid succession in Justin's eyes and on his face like the peppering spray of machine-gun fire.

Magee held her breath. As a businessman, Justin would understand why she'd stretched the truth. Wouldn't he? Of all people, surely he would realize that fine, upstanding individuals sometimes did not-so-fine-and-upstanding things in the name of business.

'Well.' He exhaled through his nostrils. 'When you confess, you really go all-out. You didn't even give me a chance to change the light bulb in my torture chamber.'

She blinked. Was he being funny or sarcastic?

In the next instant, he pulled away. Jumping out of the bed, he presented her with a view of his back as he yanked on his sweatpants.

Tears pricked her eyes. *Definitely sarcastic*.

Pulling the sheet over her breasts, she sat half-up on the bed. He faced her, his expression bleak. Shivers chilled her spine.

'Why are you telling me this now?' he asked dully.

All right, in *no* way did she hear understanding in his tone. If confession was good for the soul, she'd like to see some quick evidence, because the slippery path to hell suddenly seemed to sport a much higher grade of asphalt than did the pothole-pocked road to heaven.

'Because we're together now.' At least, she'd *thought* they'd shared something special together this week-end. Something so special that it would continue long after the Willoughbys returned to England.

Had she been wrong?

'Justin, we've made love. I couldn't keep lying to you after that.' Although she'd managed to hold out for several passionate sessions. *Ahem*.

He flipped a hand. 'I get it. You could lie to me before we started having sex, but not after.'

Her face stung. *Having sex*. Not making love. Not even the non-committal 'sleeping together.' Just raunchy, thrown-her-down-and-have-my-way-with-her sex.

She pressed her lips together. Justin was angry with her. Fair enough. He had a right to be. However, he hadn't earned the right to lecture her about lying — not with *his* track record.

* * *

Justin stared at Magee as she sat up straighter on the bed, the rumpled sheets tucked around her. Speaking slowly, she said, 'Before we made love for the first time . . . our relationship was about business. Well, it hasn't been

266

all business since we came to Whistler,' she amended. 'However, basically, until now, this whole weekend was about me helping you sign the deal with Willoughby Bikes.'

Unbelievable. He rubbed his cheek. She'd just lumped the four months since she'd contacted him about moving his advertising needs to her father's company into the same category as his desperate, last-minute bid to salvage this weekend. And what about her safety on Whistler's mountain biking trails? Hadn't she considered what might have *happened* to her?

'We're not talking about the deal, Magee. We're not talking about this weekend. We're talking about a lie you told two months ago and probably planned to tell for a good two months before that. Then you come to Whistler and hop on a bike you now admit you don't know how to ride?' He paced the bedroom. Yesterday, Magee had screamed as her bike had whipped past the Willoughbys. Her shout hadn't

267

represented her warrior cry of challenge. She hadn't been too upset or distracted by the charade to concentrate on her riding in the moment before she'd flipped into the mud.

In both cases, she'd been *terrified*.

Images of her lying bloody and broken beside her rental bike on a steep, twisting mountain trail swamped him. 'Pretending you can handle those bike trails when you can't? Not asking for tips or any sort of help?' He stopped pacing. 'You could have killed yourself. Don't you realize how lucky you are to have left that trail with a minor scrape and ruined sunglasses? You could have split your head open like a melon on those rocks.'

'I was wearing a helmet,' she sniffed with the dignity of a queen as she sat stiff-backed on the bed.

He snorted. 'A helmet isn't always enough. You could have really hurt yourself. You could have broken a bone — or your neck! What the hell was so important about landing my account that you placed your life in danger like that?'

'Does there have to be a specific reason? I wanted your account, and I would have done nearly anything to get it.' She sighed. 'You told me you needed the advantage of an account executive with mountain biking experience. You wouldn't consider moving to Sinclair otherwise. Well, with one tiny lie, you got what you wanted — in me. Granted, I didn't expect I'd *have* to learn to mountain bike so soon, or under these circumstances. I thought I could provide CycleMania with excellent service. I just needed to research a few things. Until our lunch on Wednesday, I had no trouble living up to my promises, if you'll remember.'

Her presentation had rocked. However, her work performance didn't excuse her shoddy business practices. 'And that's how you conduct your business? By lying?'

'Isn't that how you conduct yours?'

'Touché.' Clearly, the success of

Sinclair Advertising meant as much to her as expanding CycleMania did to him. Yesterday's fantasies of Magee swollen with his child returned to mock him. Only an ignorant blockhead would imagine a woman like Magee Sinclair content to sacrifice her career for the dubious honor of traipsing barefoot and pregnant around his condo kitchen while he chased the almighty buck with the same lousy ethics he'd obviously inherited from his father.

Justin had learned never to expect anything from Richard Kane. He'd required less from Tina than she'd eventually offered. He wanted too much for his business. And he'd expected more integrity from Magee than he ever had from his old man, Tina, and his own sorry ass all stuffed into the same deserved-to-be-drowned-in-it gunnysack.

Damn it.

He held out a hand. 'Magee — '

'Oh, you're a fine one to talk about lying.' Eyes blazing, she threw off the sheets and grabbed her nightgown from the bottom of the bed. Naked breasts bobbing, she scrambled off the mattress.

God, she was beautiful. And his for the taking only a few minutes ago. His for the loving.

She tugged on the nightgown over her head. The buttoned opening jammed on her crown. Buttons popped off and spit in all directions. One smacked him in the forehead, but she was too fired up to notice. Justin rubbed his stinging brow as she shoved the flannel over her legs and faced him.

'Whose idea was it that I should masquerade as Tina?' She planted her hands on flannel-swathed hips. 'Who decided we should lie to Kate and Nate, and *then*, when I suggested telling them the truth, who jumped all over me like an ant at a picnic?' Moving quicker than he'd ever seen, she snatched her tote bag off the dresser. She shook the purse at him. 'And what about the cheat sheet? Did I come up with that brainwave?' She tossed the monster-sized purse on the bed. 'If I had that stupid sheet now, I'd rip it up.'

Those damn cheat sheets. They'd been more trouble than they were worth.

'Wait.' He peered at her. When he'd tripped over her purse in the foyer, he hadn't seen the second sheet — the one he'd delivered to her apartment after she'd informed him that the sheet left in his sports jacket basically sucked. 'What do you mean, if you had the cheat sheet now? Where is it?'

'Gone.' Her eyes sparkled with defiance.

'That's not an answer. Where?'

She flicked a hand. 'A recycling bin in the Village. Kate nearly caught sight of it while we were shopping, so I got rid of it. It's probably shredded to bits by now.'

Justin ground his teeth. 'Don't you think *we* should have discussed that move first?' What kind of partnership was this?

Magee blinked away hot tears. 'Why? If I'm so good at lying, I don't need a cheat sheet to cheat the Willoughbys, do I?' She probably made no sense, but no way would she lie down and let Justin tromp all over her. He held accountability for this whole mess, too. 'Now I bet you wish I hadn't chucked it, so you could wave it in my face and tell me how to act, how to be Tina. How to lie for you. Well, guess what, Justin? A lie is a lie — no matter who lies first. A game is a game. That's what we're doing, right? Playing a game?'

'Is that what you think?' His jaw barely moved.

Cold invaded her chest. She certainly didn't want to believe their relationship meant so little to him. However, she had to consider the towering mountain of evidence. For all she knew, he'd only slept with her to help ensure the Willoughbys bought their lover cover. To manipulate her into putting her heart into her role. Her believability quotient would have shot through the roof.

'Why shouldn't I think that way?' She tented her fingers over her nose. *Don't cry!* 'Your girlfriend breaks up with you, and your only concern is how Tina's absence might affect your business deal.' She spread out her hands. 'So what do you do? Find a fake Tina the same day. A lot like shopping for shoelaces. Any brand will do. And now, unless you tell me otherwise, my guess is you'd like me to continue lying for you. To parade around as Tina, so you can clinch your deal.'

His face shuttered. 'Looks like you have me figured out.'

No denying her accusation? A sob escaped her mouth. 'Justin, that's hypocrisy.' Turning, she hugged her middle. Her shoulders hunched. 'If you don't mind, I'd like privacy before Kate and Nate return and I have to play my part again. Please take what you need from your dresser and leave.'

'Magee.' His voice was rough.

'Don't. Not another word. Just go.'

Grunting, he retrieved his clothes. His masculine scent swept around her — part musk, part woodsy spice, and all Justin. Tramping to the door, he brushed past so close that the skirt of her nightgown ruffled in his wake.

The bedroom door shut quietly behind him.

Magee stood rooted to the spot, her knuckles digging into her ribs as she rocked back and forth. Her stomach ached, her heart hurt — she couldn't breathe!

She focused her gaze on the carpet, tears searing her cheeks. She'd played Justin's game and she'd lost. Soon the Willoughbys would return, and she'd have to pretend that she and Justin were in love. Yet every time she looked at him she'd see the truth in his eyes.

He didn't want her for herself, warts and all. He only wanted her for what she could do for him — and for his precious business.

She'd fallen head over heels for a heel.

She was in love with a jerk.

★　★　★

The next three days were hell for Justin. The Magee Sinclair he knew — that lively, entertaining whirlwind he'd accidentally blackmailed into helping him dupe the Willoughbys — vanished in the aftermath of their argument Sunday morning. *Poof!* Like magic, she'd disappeared.

In her place, once she'd emerged from the bedroom after Kate and Nate returned from Garibaldi Park, he'd discovered a stiff-jointed marionette. His to pull the strings and control. To make her do as he pleased.

Except he *wasn't* pleased. Not with how she'd tricked him into becoming a client, and not with his sad lack of business ethics.

Her charge of hypocrisy haunted him as they drove back to Vancouver and ensconced the Willoughbys in a five-star hotel for the duration of their stay. The truth behind Magee's accusation dogged him Monday and Tuesday while he toured his guests around the store locations intended for the CycleMania expansion. Meanwhile, 'Tina' worked nine to five, providing Magee with a valid excuse to restrict her role to the evenings. Throughout Act Three of their poorly rehearsed stage play, she performed her part as Justin's lover with a polite detachment that escaped Kate and Nate — probably because she reserved the chief components of her new ice queen persona for *him*.

By Wednesday, Justin's conscience had suffered several thrashings. Then Tina — as in Johnston — pulled into his condo parking lot as he was leaving to pick up Magee and the Willoughbys for dinner. In a variation of Friday night in Whistler, Tina offered him 'one more chance' to take her back. Feeling like scum, he rejected her yet again.

Later, over coffee and dessert at a

popular seafood restaurant, Magee tensed whenever he held her hand. When they kissed, her lips felt cool and stiff. The passionless response following their fiery lovemaking in Whistler spoke volumes about the pain and disappointment he'd caused her.

He was disappointed, too — in himself. After everything that had happened, he still wanted the Willoughby Bikes deal. He could taste his ambition, bitter and metallic, in his mouth. However, he couldn't bear witnessing the slow drowning of Magee's spirit with every additional enactment of their ruse. And he hated conning the English couple he now admired and respected as friends as well as potential business associates.

After dinner, Nate requested a second visit to the warehouse Justin and he had toured with Justin's real estate agent earlier that morning while Kate had visited the Vancouver Art Gallery located in a historic courthouse and 'Tina' was 'busy' working. Justin contacted Celia Watts, the agent, and arranged a meeting at the empty warehouse.

Celia let in the group with the lockbox key, then remained in the front office glued to her cell phone while Justin paraded his troops up and down the echoing concrete aisles. Both Kate and Nate raved over Justin's choice of the rental site as a distribution center for the Western Canada leg of Willoughby Bikes' assault on the North American market. In a recap of the last three days, Nate said only good things about the deal.

'Yes, we very much like what we have seen of the cycling trade in the Vancouver area, Justin. Wouldn't you say so, Kate?' Nate looped an arm around his smiling wife. 'I shan't speak for my father, of course. However, considering the advantages of your proposal coupled with my recommendation, I'd wager he won't argue.'

'Too right,' Kate asserted with her customary verve.

The couple's easy rapport ate at

Justin. The woman standing rigidly by *his* side, her hand a frigid ball in his, could take lessons from Kate Willoughby in how to support and cheer on her man.

If only he could *be* Magee's man.

Fat chance now.

The chill of the cool warehouse rushed over him, and he pasted on a smile for his guests. Too many opposing thoughts crammed his brain. Primarily, why *should* Magee feel anything but rancor toward him and his achievements? He was every bit the hypocrite she'd claimed, condemning her actions while pulling a major scam of his own. Suddenly, considering he'd waited months to receive Nate's blessing, the prospect of clinching the Willoughby Bikes deal no longer held the same appeal as it had seven days ago.

Justin still wanted to succeed, but based on his merits, not his shortcomings. And certainly not at the risk of diminishing himself further in Magee's eyes.

'Um, Nate, we haven't discussed advertising strategy. You remember the account executive I mentioned?'

Magee's cold fingers stiffened like shards of ice against his palm. She cut him a swift and deadly glance, as if he were too dense to realize he was turning the tap of ruination wide open and willingly washing his dreams for CycleMania down the drain.

Nate stroked his chin. 'Ah, yes, the advertising representative. Maggie St. Claire, was it?'

'Magee,' Justin corrected. 'Pronounced like the surname: M-a-g-e-e. Magee Sinclair.' A name as charmingly different as the woman.

'Justin, don't,' she croaked, eyes huge.

'Right,' Nate responded. 'Magee Sinclair. Good thinking, Justin. We should meet her before we leave. Kate has a few ideas we wouldn't mind incorporating into the adverts. Could you arrange a meeting for the morrow?'

'I can arrange a meeting for right

now.' Looking first Kate and then Nate in the eyes, he gestured to Magee. 'Kathryn and Nathan Willoughby, I'd like to introduce Magee Sinclair of Sinclair Advertising.'

Kate laughed, the melodious sound boomeranging off the high warehouse ceiling. 'Justin, you're having us on, aren't you? How absolutely sweet! How could our Tina possibly be this Magee person? She's our Tina.'

'No, she isn't Tina,' Justin reiterated.

'Pardon?' Kate's forehead wrinkled.

Magee's gaze lowered. 'Justin's right,' she said quietly. 'I'm not Tina Johnston. I'm sorry for trying to fool you.'

'What are you on about?' Nate asked. 'If Tina isn't — if *you* aren't Tina, then who is?'

Behind them, the metal warehouse door banged shut and the rapid clacking of high heels echoed against the concrete floor.

Two pairs of high heels.

Justin turned. Celia Watts scampered behind a rampaging redhead.

'I'm sorry, Mr. Kane!' Celia wailed. 'She barged in! I don't even know who she is!'

'I do,' Kate stated simply. 'Or, I can guess. Tina-Jo . . . er, Tina Johnston, I presume?'

'You bet your biscuits, sister.' Tina smirked. 'And do I have a tale to tell you.' She glared at Justin. 'Blocking my number on your cell phone can't stop me, you stupid jerk. Who do you think you're dealing with?'

'Wait a minute!' He threw out his hands. 'This is *my* confession!'

No one listened. Five different voices pelted him with demands and questions.

Pandemonium ensued.

11

'Sounds great, Dad.' Magee affected a cheerful voice as she spoke into her father's desk phone. Rubbing her forehead, she swiveled back and forth in his leather chair. Her thighs were jumping as if she'd knocked back ten energy drinks. She'd moved her laptop, tablet, briefcase, and several files into her dad's office this morning. After Justin's unexpected confession last night and the resulting meltdown with Nathan Willoughby, she needed the privacy her father's office provided so she could push the disastrous weekend out of her mind and re-evaluate her plan for pulling the advertising agency out of the red.

Namely, pursuing new and far less frustrating clients.

'You and Mom can stay at the lake as

long as you want,' she continued. 'Don't even think about the agency. No emails, no texts. I can handle anything that comes up.' A radical overstatement. However, she wasn't about to ruin her parents' first vacation in years with the news that she and Justin had destroyed any chance of Willoughby Bikes doing business with either CycleMania or Sinclair Advertising.

She'd tell her dad everything upon his return — and steel herself to face the consequences. If she had to relinquish her promotion to account director, she would. If she had to find a new *job*, she would.

Whatever it took to regain her father's faith in her.

'Say hi to Mom for me,' she finished, then said goodbye and hung up. On her laptop, she opened a spreadsheet titled Potential Clients.

A knock came at the office door. Magee glanced up. 'Yes?'

Tommy, the agency gopher, entered. 'Hi, Magee.' Tommy held a bundle. 'I didn't know if I should buzz you first or — ?'

She shook her head. 'No need for buzzing. I'm not confiscating my father's office, Tommy. I just have a lot of work.'

Tommy lifted a hand. 'You don't have to explain to me.' He approached the desk. 'A package arrived for you from Mrs. Rubens's Rip 'N' Stitch.' He placed the bundle on the desk. 'Plus, I ran into Patti. She asked me to give you this.' He handed Magee a folded message slip.

'Thanks.' The tiny piece of paper chafed her fingertips.

'I don't know why she can't use email like everyone else.' Tommy adjusted the button on his long shirtsleeve.

'I do.' The slips of pink message paper were twelve thousand times more annoying than email, and Patti loved to exasperate Magee. The condescending notes had proliferated since her return from Whistler.

With a few taps on her keyboard,

Magee could easily delay responding to an internal memo. However, no such impersonal option existed when Patti dropped off a physical note and practically dared Magee to read and respond to it in the infernal woman's presence.

Tommy left the office, closing the door.

Sighing, Magee scanned Patti's breathless prose: *Blah, blah . . . too many accounts for you to handle . . . if you can't manage them all, I can . . . blah . . . happy to take over any time . . . blah, blah, more of the same.*

Magee stuffed the note into a large envelope in her briefcase. Someday she'd use her collection of holier-than-thou 'suggestions' received over the last six months to create a giant papier maché Patti piñata. Magee would fill her masterpiece with Purdy's chocolates and take great delight in bashing it to bits.

However, at the moment, she couldn't

bear to think about Patti Slotnik. She couldn't bear to think about Justin, either, but the delivery from Mrs. Rubens forced her to.

The package could only contain his repaired sports jacket. Magee had asked Mrs. Rubens to courier the jacket to Justin's office and then bill Magee. Clearly, the seamstress hadn't recalled the instructions. Or she'd mixed them up. Maybe she'd billed Justin.

Wouldn't that beat all?

Magee touched the brown paper package, and sadness flooded her. She missed him. She had it bad. A few hours away from the guy and she craved the sound of his voice, his touch.

Her smartphone, lying on the desktop, rang. She glanced at the incoming number. *Justin Kane.*

Voice hollow, she answered. 'Hello?'

'I'm driving the Willoughbys to the airport,' he informed her without preamble. 'Nate changed their flight.'

'They're leaving today?' A day early.

'Yeah.' His deep voice sounded flat. 'I

tried talking Nate out of it, but he wouldn't listen.'

Gee, I wonder why?

'Frankly, I'm surprised Nate agreed to let either of us drive them.' Magee picked up a pen and twirled it between her fingers. 'Wouldn't they rather use a limo service?'

'I insisted,' Justin replied.

Of course he had.

She drummed the pen on the desk. Back and forth, back and forth. Like a juiced-up rock star.

She drew in a breath. Last night at the warehouse, when Justin began revealing her identity, she'd honestly thought he'd changed his mind about continuing the charade. For an instant, she hadn't wanted him to confess at all. Despite her objections to perpetuating the lie, she'd wanted his plan to succeed . . . because she loved him.

Then Tina had stormed in with a story about tailing the group throughout the evening. Apparently, Tina had spent hours gathering her courage to

289

expose Justin and Magee. That Justin had blocked the woman's cell number while they were in Whistler and then rejected her in his condo parking lot before dinner had catapulted the redhead into bunny-boiling mode.

Magee chewed her lip. Had Justin anticipated Tina's parking-lot stalking? Had he decided to come clean at the warehouse only so he could beat Tina to the punch, thereby saving face with Kate and Nate?

Believing such an awful thing about the man Magee loved hurt. Enormously. However, she couldn't see her way through this latest snafu to believing anything else.

'Magee?' Justin asked over the cell. 'My line is clear. Are you there?'

She tossed down the pen. 'You're driving the Willoughbys to the airport,' she reiterated. 'I'm guessing you'd like me to come along.'

'Well, yes.'

'Why? Justin, what would be the point? I've already apologized to Kate and Nate twice. There's nothing left to say. We blew it.' She hesitated. 'Unless . . . do you think if I helped you butter them up during the drive, Nate will come around and commit to the deal?'

'No! Why are you so eager to believe the worst of me? I said it last night and I'll say it again, I'm sorry. I'm sorry about Kate and Nate, and I'm sorry about us, too.' His voice softened. 'I want to see you again.'

Butterflies fluttered in her chest. A Justin-fix would feel so good. Just one little fix.

She blinked. One little fix sounded an awful lot like one little lie. One white lie that led to two, then three, then four, then sixty.

To a hundred harmful, noxious lies.

She straightened in her father's chair. 'I can't face Kate and Nate right now.' *I can't face you.* In Whistler, she'd told Justin it didn't matter who'd lied first. However, he might have abandoned his scheme to con the Willoughbys if she hadn't been so quick to cover her ass and agree to help him in the first place. 'I'm sorry, Justin, but I can't.'

A heavy silence stretched between them. 'You can be so damn stubborn.'

'At least I'm good at something.' Disconnecting, she turned off her phone. If he tried again, he'd go straight to voice mail. Those were messages she *could* delete.

Delete, delete, delete.

Nothing left.

Like her empty heart.

★　★　★

'Hold my calls, Agnes,' Justin instructed as he strode past his executive assistant's desk. Yanking open his office door, he glanced back. 'Did you get that?'

'Yes, sir,' the middle-age woman responded. 'A package arrived while you were out. It's on your desk.'

'Thank you.' Inside his office, Justin shut the door and dropped the blinds on the window overlooking Agnes's station. A hand on his hip, he pinched the bridge of his nose. Would the thumping in his forehead never end?

Driving the Willoughbys to the airport had resulted in a big fat lack of progress. Throughout the trip, Nate had maintained an overly quiet demeanor while Kate had chattered incessantly about nothing. Worse, Magee's remark on the phone regarding Justin's motivation for driving the Willoughbys had found its mark. Until she'd mentioned buttering up Nate, Justin hadn't realized his insistence on seeing off the Willoughbys might have sprung from a deep-rooted need to pursue his goals at all costs.

Well, if he'd subconsciously intended to charm Nate into giving CycleMania another chance, he'd failed. The Englishman's mind was made up. Unless time, distance, and a minor miracle altered Nate's perspective, Justin had no hope of securing the Willoughby Bikes distributorship.

In the end, he'd offered to email

Nate a list of other industry contacts. Not that Justin's recommendation meant anything at this point, and Nate probably possessed several contacts already, but Justin had — again — insisted. *Shit.*

He sat at his desk and rummaged through the top drawer for a bottle of ibuprofen. The bulky courier package Agnes had mentioned hulked behind his computer. Justin dragged the package toward him. As he popped the bottle cap, he read the 'From' field on the package label: *Mrs. Rubens's Rip 'N'Stitch, via Sinclair Advertising.*

Below the label, Magee's flowing handwriting stated, 'Your sports jacket.'

He crunched a tablet between his teeth. Three measly words? That was it? He swallowed the tablet chunks without water, the medication sour on his tongue. Magee's contempt for his behavior rang through the simplicity of her note. She had shut right down on him. Even last night, when Tina had burst into the warehouse, Magee's reticent expression had said it all.

From what Justin had pieced together, Magee was under the impression that he'd realized Tina was following them. And, possibly, after he'd rejected Tina in his condo parking lot, he should have guessed she'd retaliate. However, considering his sincere apology in Whistler for unintentionally hurting her, he hadn't anticipated she would appear yet again and trash him out of sheer spite.

And then there was Magee . . . the most confusing and fascinating woman he'd met in his life. What had she said on the phone? *At least I'm good at something.* What did that mean?

He shoved the pill bottle back into his desk drawer. Sometimes Magee's nerves or spontaneity got the better of her, but did she really think she was a screw-up? She'd had him convinced she mountain biked as a hobby. Even in Whistler, when she'd handled the bike like a novice on the easy trail, he'd thought her stress over duping the Willoughbys was responsible.

And the way she'd managed to pull

off 'being' Tina for several days certainly testified to her ability to think on her feet.

So. Either Magee Sinclair didn't give herself enough credit, or the woman was such an accomplished liar that Justin didn't know her at all.

His gut clenched. *You know the truth*. The Magee Sinclair who'd held herself responsible for his torn sports jacket possessed a generous heart, a Jiminy Cricket-schooled conscience, and a natural inclination to help others . . . but maybe not a whole lot of self-confidence.

He picked up the courier package. Memories of their kiss on English Bay Beach, when she'd lost her balance on the drift log, rushed over him. A joy he'd never before experienced filled him. In the next instant, an excruciating pain lanced his chest.

Emotions. Hell. Who knew they could drive so deep?

He pushed aside the package, then got up and carried it to a file cabinet. Standing at the tower of drawers, he stared at the wrapping.

Obviously, he needed to come to terms with his feelings for Magee. As much as it hurt, however, he had to examine his own psyche first. He owed that much to Magee, and he owed it to himself.

Otherwise, he couldn't move forward. And he wanted to.

He wanted a future, a family, a life.

With every fiber of his being, he needed the woman at the core of it all.

His gaze lingered on the package. Longing swept through him.

But he wouldn't open it.

Not yet.

★　★　★

'*Then* what do I find when I arrive at work this morning? Another snide note from Patti Slotnik on my father's desk!' Wielding her fork, Magee punctured a spear of broccoli in the mound of chop suey on her plate. Susannah sat cross-legged on the floor on the opposite side of the coffee table. Beside Magee on the rattan love seat, Monster purred. The presence of her friend and the friendly co-op cat should calm her. However, in the eight lousy days since Justin had asked her to accompany him and the Willoughbys to the airport, her irritation with *every facet of her life* hadn't abated one iota. She couldn't even trust her stupid reflexes with chopsticks.

'Ugh, how irritating.' Susannah gracefully maneuvered her chopsticks to retrieve a morsel of almond chicken. Despite the sticky-hot humidity hovering in Magee's living room, Susannah remained unruffled. A serene blond Buddha without the belly.

Magee chewed and swallowed the broccoli. 'You know, I've received one note from Patti per day during this week alone. I can barely survive PMS. Now I'm stuck with PSS. Patti Ever-lovin' Slotnik Syndrome.'

Susannah smiled. 'Actually, that's P-E-S-S, if you go with the Ever-lovin' in the middle. PESS.'

Magee giggled. No matter how crappy her day, her week — her life — her friend helped her feel better.

'Make that *pest*.' She speared another broccoli chunk. 'Seriously, Susannah, the woman drives me nuts. I know she's been with the ad agency longer than I have, and she's had more success with her accounts lately, too. But does she have to rub it in?'

Susannah sipped her lite beer. 'She's not rubbing, Magee. She's trying to get under your skin. The question is, why do you let her?'

Magee sighed. 'I don't know. She makes me feel undeserving.'

'Only because you *let* her.' Susannah set down her bottle. 'Honey, we've been through this. Sinclair Advertising is a family business. Your grandfather started the company, after all. From what you've told me, Patti knew the score when she was hired. Given the company history, once you came onboard, it only made sense that your father would groom *you* for account director. Someday you'll run the place. You have to gain your experience at the pace he determines. If Patti can't accept that, she should find another job.'

'Yeah, but — '

Susannah waved her chopsticks. 'Even Yeah-But and Costello could see their way through this mess. If you want to become account director, you have to show Patti who's boss. Have faith in yourself, old buddy, old pal. How can you expect Patti to have faith in you when *you* don't? The same goes for your dad and even Justin.'

'Justin's not in the picture.' Magee ate the broccoli and poked a chunk of bok choy.

Susannah's cheeks glowed. 'Um, I said too much.' She scooped pork fried rice onto her chopsticks.

Magee looked at her. 'Susannah? Spill. I haven't mentioned Justin in days.' She'd only dreamt and thought and obsessed about him every minute. 'Tonight is my turn to whine and dine.

I choose the topics and vent until I'm done. So why bring him up?'

Susannah cleared her throat. 'He's been on my mind.'

'Then take him off it!'

Susannah laughed. 'No, not in that way. I had lunch with him today.'

'You did what?' The bok choy bounced off Magee's fork and plopped onto Monster's head. The cat blinked his amber eyes and meowed.

'Oh, Monster! Baby, I'm sorry!' Against the soundtrack of Susannah's continuing chuckles, Magee snatched the bok choy with a paper napkin and wiped the cat's head.

Monster dashed off the cushion and hid under the love seat. Abandoning her dinner, Magee bent on one knee and retrieved the cat.

Sitting on the love seat again, she asked Susannah, 'Did he call you?' She stroked Monster's soft fur until he purred again.

Susannah nodded. 'What could I do? The guy sounded miserable.' She ate her pork fried rice. 'We had a nice lunch. He's in a tough place right now, Magee, trying to make sense of what happened between you two and why.' Her chopsticks tap-danced against her plate, her gaze riveted to her task. 'Anyway, I kind of like him now. He's still a little uptight, but he's not a jerk of the first order like that cheating slime, Brent Doyle. The way I see it, Justin Kane's a good guy who got caught up in his ambition. The poor S.O.B. wants to learn from his mistakes.'

Magee gawked at her friend. In the last eight days, she hadn't heard one word from Justin. Not a syllable. At the least, she'd expected him to call her at work and fire her. The Willoughby Bikes deal was history, but CycleMania's local advertising needs remained. After her lie about the mountain biking, why would he want her to continue handling his account?

Even Patti, despite her annoying imperfections, could manage Justin's

302

business needs with more grace.

Yet, so far, he *hadn't* fired Magee. Apparently, instead he'd chosen to keep her on pins and needles while he'd poured out his guts to her friend.

Susannah, who knew *far* too much about her.

Hugging Monster close, Magee narrowed her eyes. 'Okay, Susannah, what did you tell him?'

★ ★ ★

'After all these years, your mother refuses to accept that the practice must come first.' Justin's father paced the law-book-lined study. 'I try, son. God knows I try. But I can't be in two places at once, and the client's needs must be satisfied. A man has to prioritize, damn it!' His index finger stabbed the air.

Seated on the leather couch, Justin nursed his scotch. He knew this scene inside-out, upside down, and sideways. He should. He'd seen it played out countless times in his childhood . . .

although, at ten, he'd been minus the booze.

As Richard Kane's eldest son, Justin's role during his father's frequent performances was to listen, to absorb the crumbs of wisdom his father chose to impart, and thereby to learn.

'I don't know, Dad. Mom has a point. I mean, David didn't even show tonight. I know he's around. I spoke to him this morning.' On any given weekend, unless one of the three brothers needed to go out of town, missing a Kane Sunday dinner was taboo. Only their father possessed the latitude to pop in and out like a visiting dignitary. 'So why didn't Dave come?' Justin sipped his scotch. 'He figured things would wind up like always. Mom perfecting the silent treatment. You storming. Me sitting here.' Taking it all in. 'Dad, it's bad enough when you promise Mom you'll make up for the missed family dinners and interrupted weekends, but now Trevor is pulling the same crap on *his* family.'

Justin's father glared at him. 'Trevor knows what the law firm means to me.'

'Can't argue with you there.' Halfway through dessert, while Trevor's wife was breastfeeding their infant daughter in a bedroom, Trevor had awarded Justin the responsibility of driving his niece and sister-in-law home. Without consulting Brandi, Trevor had raced back to Kane, Kane & Associates to slave over the tax law case that had catapulted their father's blood pressure into the stratosphere. 'Is this the sort of life you want for Trev? Or for Brandi and little Michelle?' Justin swept a hand around his father's shrine to his career — the study. 'A kid deserves to have her dad around when he says he'll be there, even if she is only eight weeks old.'

'What would you know about it?' his father blustered. 'You don't have a family. Thirty-five, and you're still single. What scares off the women? Something wrong with the swimmers?'

'My swimmers are fine.' Justin plunked his scotch glass on the

305

mahogany coffee table. He hoped they were fine! 'By the way, thank you for the fear-mongering. It helps me sleep at night, knowing you'll never change.' *But I can.*

They tossed barbs back and forth a while longer, until Brandi poked her head into the study, arms cradling a drowsy baby. Justin kissed his mother goodnight, then dropped off his sister-in-law and niece using the CycleMania van.

Now, alone in his condo, he shoved his hands into his pants pockets and stared at the glittering night view of Coal Harbor. Magee thought she was a screw-up? One visit to the Kane household would offer her a fresh perspective. She might have done the wrong thing in lying to Justin about the mountain biking, but her intentions regarding her father's advertising agency were honorable. Justin's lunch with Susannah on Friday had peeled his eyes wide open. He hadn't invited Susannah to lunch to snoop into

Magee's motives. He'd needed clarity on the mess *he'd* created, and he'd hoped Magee's friend could offer some insight.

Well, Susannah had. Insight about himself *and* about Magee.

In Whistler, he'd sensed Magee was hiding more than her unfamiliarity with mountain biking. Thanks to Susannah's eagerness to clear her friend, he now knew what and why. He just didn't know what to do about it. For once in his life, he didn't know how to proceed. If Magee learned he'd become acquainted with her problems at the advertising agency, she might think he'd decided to continue doing business with her out of pity.

Nothing was farther from the truth. Magee loved her job, and she deserved a chance at success.

Besides, she might feel disgusted with him, but he loved her. He really did. He loved the whirlwind, he loved the chaos, he loved the sexy, cute, perky, pretty, quirky woman.

God, he missed her and the laughter she'd brought into his life. He even missed the aggravation.

More than anything, he wanted her back.

Grunting, he turned away from the window. The framed poster of the Cyclone — Willoughby's pro-level mountain bike that Magee had planned to feature in the magazine ads — stared at him from the granite breakfast bar. He'd brought the poster home from the office on Friday, the day of his and Susannah's lunch. Before meeting Susannah at the restaurant, he'd severed the threads of the dead-in-the-water deal: the renting of the warehouse and the intended new locations of more CycleMania stores. Without the Western Canada distributorship and the exclusive dealership rights for the greater Vancouver area, he couldn't accomplish the expansion in his original four-month time frame. The poster hanging in his office had only mocked him and his ludicrous master life plan.

Yet, far more than the poster, another item on the breakfast bar beckoned. The courier package which, also until Friday, he'd stored on top of his filing cabinet. After talking to Susannah, he'd opened the package. His sports jacket had lain within. However, one whiff of Magee's sweet scent — intermixed with a hint of pinot gris and Possessed — carrying from the garment had stopped him, and he'd stuffed it back into the wrapping. He hadn't been able to handle the reminder of the happiness he and Magee had shared . . . and then had so quickly lost.

He huffed out a breath. *No more wallowing, Kane.* He liked that sports jacket. He wanted to wear it again.

Stepping to the breakfast bar, he ripped into the wrapping. The sports jacket tumbled onto the granite. As he lifted the jacket, his fingers nudged a lump in the inside chest pocket. Carefully, he withdrew Magee's wispy shawl thing, the one she'd worn when the waiter had spilled the wine at The Dock. The delicate silk had dried to a stiff, crunchy texture in several places. Magee must have been so concerned about taking his sports jacket to her seamstress that she'd neglected to retrieve her belongings.

He buried his nose in the silk and inhaled. *Magee.*

Well, Magee and stagnant pinot gris.

He'd gladly accept the latter if he were guaranteed the former.

Fw . . . fwish . . . Fwick.

He peered at the folded piece of paper that had fallen out of the jacket onto the engineered hardwood.

The cheat sheet! The original he'd pushed on Magee during their stroll on English Bay Beach. That was right, when he'd picked her up for the Whistler trip, she'd mentioned forgetting the first cheat sheet in his jacket pocket.

He placed the sports jacket and wrapping on the counter. Bending, he retrieved the cheat sheet. His fingers, upon meeting the paper, tingled. *A lie is a lie, no matter who lies first.* The words Magee had tossed at him in Whistler reverberated in his brain.

He sighed. The cheat sheet was filled with lies. Lies disguised as facts fashioned into a clever mask designed for the sole purpose of promoting his business.

As he stared at the sheet, his gut roiled. He was no better than his father. No better than the man who'd bluffed his way through Justin's childhood, making promises he couldn't keep to a wife and three little boys.

Promises and lies.

He crumpled the cheat sheet and tossed it in a corner. The worst mistake of his life blared in his head like someone shouting at him through a megaphone. He'd so wanted *not* to model himself after his father that he'd wound up accomplishing a sort of modeling in reverse. He'd thought he could partition his life — business first, marriage later. And, in doing so, he wouldn't sacrifice one for the other.

He dragged his fingernails along the five o'clock shadow speckling his jaw. Man, had he been wrong. Going full bore with CycleMania hadn't gotten him anywhere, hadn't earned him anything other than a pair of leather blinders.

In the process, he'd hurt and misled a lot of people. Tina, the Willoughbys.

Magee topped the list.

Grabbing the sports jacket laced with her unique scent, he slipped one arm into a sleeve, then pushed in the other. His left hand jammed in the sleeve. *What the hell?*

He sloughed off the jacket and examined Mrs. Rubens's repairs. Or, as it appeared, her *lack* of repairs. Had Magee hired a half-blind seamstress? The left sleeve was sewn clear through the seam.

Justin chuckled. How like Magee to hire a seamstress who, considering this example of Mrs. Rubens's skills, was probably in dire need of the work.

Yep, that would be just like Magee. A total reflection of the tenderhearted woman he loved — and had no intention of losing.

Throwing back his head, he laughed.

12

At eleven Monday morning, Magee strolled into her father's office with something approaching a skip in her step. Her breakfast meeting with Angela Chamberlain of Ultra-Chic Hair Designs had fared better than she'd dared to imagine. Angela had gushed over the copy the Creative team had drafted for local radio spots, and the competitive drive-time hours indicated in Magee's media plan perfectly targeted Angela's clientele of professional urban women. Even the local Internet and print ads were motoring along. For once, Magee had the golden touch.

She sat at her dad's desk and pulled in the chair, spine straight. She refused to allow any mistakes to occur with Ultra-Chic. She would not lose the agency another client.

She reached for her father's appointment book. Following his custom, she'd record the essentials of her meeting with Angela so he could easily catch up in a manner familiar to him upon his return next week.

As she flipped the pages to today's date, a message slip sailed off the top cover. *Patti*. Would the woman never give up?

Pressing her lips together, Magee snatched the missive. So much for her fleeting bubble of happiness. Aside from this morning's success with Ultra-Chic, the last five days since the warehouse debacle had been awful. In other words, her personal life sucked. On Friday, Susannah had informed Justin that the mountain biking lie was Susannah's brainwave. While Magee's friend had meant well, admitting the whole pathetic story should have been Magee's call. Instead, her friend had felt it necessary to take up her cause . . . as if she were a lost cause.

Besides, Magee had reasons for not

telling him. Namely, she hadn't wanted him to believe she was trying to excuse her actions. She'd been wrong to lie, plain and simple.

Gripping Patti's note, Magee pushed back the chair. Apparently, she didn't have to worry about Justin Kane offering her absolution. Regardless of Susannah's efforts, he still hadn't contacted Magee. But then, she hadn't emailed or called him, either. She couldn't. Her humiliation cut too deeply.

However, this . . . She scrunched the memo paper. *This* she could handle.

She should have done so months ago.

Note in her fist, she marched out of her dad's office and toward Patti's cubicle. Along the way, she ran into Tommy returning from the photocopier room with a sheaf of papers. 'Hi, Tommy. Is Patti at her desk?'

He nodded. 'At her desk, away from her desk, at her desk, away again. She looks kind of green today. Definitely in a bad mood. You might want to avoid her.'

'Thanks, but not this time. We're having it out.'

'Go, Magee!'

Reaching Patti's desk, Magee discovered her fellow account executive 'away again.' Crossing her arms over her suit jacket, she tapped her foot. Patti's computer hummed on the desk, the monitor displaying what looked like a custom screensaver featuring a cartoon shark circling a freaked-out female skin diver. The snorkeler's short yellow hair stood up, her green eyes huge behind her swim mask.

Magee leaned closer. *That's me!*

Her hand jerked, bumping the mouse. The screensaver blinked off to reveal the file Patti had been working on. A media plan.

But not just any media plan. *Magee's* media plan — for Ultra-Chic Hair Designs. The one she'd shown to Angela forty minutes ago.

Crap! How had Patti accessed her files? Magee's accounts were password protected on the agency's internal network. She changed the password every few weeks and taped it to the back panel of her top left-hand desk draw —

Ohhhh. Crrrrap.

Patti had found the password. Why was she digging around in Magee's files?

Tossing the memo on the desk, Magee sat at the computer and examined the file. It wasn't unusual for a client to request changes, but evidently Patti had replaced the drive-time hours Magee had promised Angela with . . . polka hours?

Angela would have a conniption if she saw these changes! As a result, Magee could lose the Ultra-Chic account.

An eerie tingle seized her spine. The Sear-Soothe and Barnacle Beer catastrophes — all these months, Magee had assumed *she* was responsible. Now . . . she blinked . . . had Patti sabotaged her accounts?

How could the woman accomplish such a thing when both the client and

Magee needed to sign off on changes? Unless . . .

Heart pounding, she snatched a notepad beside the keyboard and grabbed a pencil from the ceramic holder. As she scribbled on the pad, several attempts at forging her signature appeared.

'Magee? What do you think you're doing?'

Patti. The snake.

Magee whirled on the chair. 'What do you think *you're* doing? Sabotaging my accounts, Patti?' She stood. 'Call me naive, I never dreamed you'd stoop so low.'

Tommy had been right — Patti looked green. Physically ill. Beads of sweat dotted the woman's forehead, and her brown hair hung in lank strings around her square face.

'It's not what you think.' Patti clutched her stomach.

'It's exactly what I think.' Magee waved the notepad. 'Forging my signature? Patti, really. I have quite a collection of these.' She grabbed the message slip off the desk and jammed it into her suit jacket pocket. 'Mighty fine evidence, I'd say. Confess. It's good for the soul. Believe me, I should know.'

Patti's sweaty face paled. 'I feel awful. I need to go home. I've been barfing bacon and eggs.' She moaned. 'The bacon was only a week past the expiration date.'

Ugh. Magee aimed the notepad at her suspect. 'You're not going any-where.'

'Magee, I have to puke!'

'Then spill — with the truth.' A crowd began assembling around them, including Tommy, but Magee remained focused on her mission. 'Or, I swear, I'll let you get sick right here.'

'All right!' Patti wiped her nose. 'I have some ideas for Ultra-Chic. I planned to show them to you this afternoon. Honest.'

Magee snorted. 'I may be naive, but I'm not stupid.' She pointed at the monitor. 'This isn't an idea. It's sabotage. How far does it extend?'

Patti hunched over, hugging her stomach. 'Just the billboards and the beer ad. I authorized a few changes.' Another moan.

'*A few?*' Magee poked Patti's shoulder with the pad. 'What else?'

Her adversary managed a weak grin. 'It was so easy. You didn't suspect a thing. You don't deserve that promotion, Ms. Nepotism. I do. Sooner or later, your father would have realized that.'

Patti had revealed her motive. Still holding the pad, Magee crossed her arms. 'Well, unfortunately for you, Ms. Slotnik, you'll never make account director at this agency. You're fired. Get out.'

'I can't leave *now*,' Patti whined. 'I need to barf.'

'Tommy will stand outside the ladies room while you do. Then he'll help you collect your things and take you home. I never want to see you in these offices again.'

Tommy escorted Patti to the wash-rooms, and the crowd cheered. At Magee's bidding, her colleagues dispersed, returning to work. Sitting at Patti's station, Magee collected all the evidence of sabotage she could find, then returned to her father's office and assembled a file for his perusal.

One week until his return, now that he'd extended his vacation. She'd best post Patti's job vacancy right away. She couldn't allow her father to pick up the pieces of a situation which she, as the future account director, should rightfully handle. And she *could* handle it — both the fallout of Patti's sabotage and the promotion.

She released a breath. It looked like she wasn't as big a screw-up as she'd thought. Discovering Patti's sabotage proved that. And, regardless of her reckless haste in choosing to masquerade as Tina, she'd pulled off the role. Furthermore, she'd fired Patti without thinking twice. She not only wanted the promotion, she'd fight for it if necessary.

What about Justin?

She moistened her lips. If she could fight for the advertising agency, then she could fight for the man she loved. No more berating herself over the mistakes she'd made — or thought she'd made. It was time to take charge.

Picking up the phone, she punched in his office number. The line was busy, and his assistant put her on hold. After an interminable minute ticked past, he answered.

'Magee,' he said, voice gruff. 'I've been trying to reach you.'

Her heart raced. Had he arrived at the same conclusion she had?

'I'm sorry. I should have contacted you before now.'

'We need to talk.' He paused. 'About business.'

Her throat squeezed.

'We have a problem.'

'Oh.' She got it. He was finally firing

323

her. What had taken so long?

'I'd like to discuss the situation right away.'

'Of course,' she responded flatly. 'Shoot.'

'Not over the phone. Here, in my office. This is a priority issue for me.'

'Right. I'll be there in twenty minutes.'

She hung up. Elbows on the desk, she steepled her fingers. No problem, she could handle this. She could handle anything Justin dished out. He could fire her if he wanted. He could pretend nothing existed between them but the remnants of their failed charade. However, she had different ideas, and she wouldn't be swayed.

She wouldn't leave his office without telling him she loved him.

*   *   *

Justin returned the cordless to its charger. He'd just tricked Magee into coming to his office. He should feel guilty. But mostly he felt smug.

He'd set a trap for the woman he loved. What did that say about him? That he still had some growing to do?

Probably. The point was, he was trying.

Having witnessed the depth of Magee's dedication to Sinclair Advertising, he'd gambled she wouldn't refuse a meeting with her father's business at stake. He'd been right.

Locking his fingers behind his head, he leaned back in his chair. In twenty minutes, his life would change for the better . . . or for the worse. His hopes rode on the better. His visit with his father last night had hit him hard. He'd barely slept afterward.

Maybe soon he could do his old man a good turn and return the favor. Teach Richard Kane a few lessons about promises and priorities. Encourage his father to repair the damage he'd caused his family before more grandchildren came along.

Justin squared his shoulders. His

father's approach to life had finally taught him something positive. He no longer needed the Willoughby Bikes deal to make him happy. Nor did he need the CycleMania expansion. He'd love to achieve those goals, but he didn't need them. He only needed Magee and the life he wanted to build with her. His future wife and children were his priority. Any success in business he managed to attain would be gravy.

He had a brand new, spanking clean, master life plan.

However, he still lacked the primary ingredient to make the plan work. Magee.

Unlacing his fingers, he straightened in his chair. A moment later, he drummed the desktop. Without Magee at his side, was he destined to become a smudged photocopy of his father?

'No,' he said aloud. No matter what Magee said or did when she arrived, he had to change his life. Starting now.

He glanced at his watch. Sixteen more minutes.

His palms began to sweat.

* * *

Breath hitching, Magee entered Justin's office. He sat leaning forward in his chair, hands laced on his desk, his shirtsleeves rolled up and his collar unbuttoned. Gazing at her.

In all the months she'd known him, she'd never seen him in a business setting without a tie. He looked incredibly hot — and she wasn't thinking beach temps.

His mouth crooked in a sexy half-smile, and her heart raced. Whatever came of this meeting, she loved him. She always would.

'Please lock the door.' He rose and stepped out from behind the desk. 'I don't want anyone disturbing us.'

He required a locked door to axe her? She glanced at the window blinds separating his office from the outer area. Also closed. She swallowed. She needed to allow the next few minutes to unfold naturally, let Justin say what he wanted. She'd take her medicine like a big girl, then hopefully knock his socks off by telling him that it didn't matter if he moved his advertising to another agency. She loved and wanted him, anyway.

If their relationship had to end, at least it would end with the truth.

She locked the door.

'You asked to see me.' She faced him.

He nodded. 'I did.'

She rubbed a clammy hand on her skirt. Stepping toward him, she placed her purse on the visitor's chair. Justin's repaired sports jacket hung on the back. Memories of their practice date crashed into her: their amazing first kiss, his hand caressing her calf, his thumb gently brushing her scratched toe.

'You received my package. Did Mrs. Rubens do a good job?' she asked. His gaze tracked her movements as he neared her, and her fingers twitched. 'I only wonder because she's in her final year of business. Her eyesight is failing, but she needs the work until her pension kicks in.'

He chuckled. 'I hope she appreciates your loyalty.'

'Why? Is something wrong?' Magee lifted the sleeve to check the repairs.

'Not a thing.' Justin grabbed the sleeve. 'Mrs. Rubens did a great job. I plan on using her myself from now on.'

His husky voice whispered up Magee's spine. 'Then what is it? On the phone, you said we have a problem.'

'We sure do.' His blue eyes darkened.

She sucked in a breath. 'Justin, this is torture. Why keep me in suspense? If you want to break off your dealings with my ad agency, just do it.'

'I don't want to terminate our dealings. I'd sure like to cement them, though.'

He didn't make sense. She jabbed his chest. 'Don't play games with me, bucko. I've made my share of mistakes, but I'm trying to resolve them and I'm ready to move forward. Can you say the same?'

'Yes.' He caught her finger. 'This isn't a game to me, either, Magee. I've never been more serious.'

She blinked. 'Then what's the problem?'

'This.' He kissed the tip of her finger. 'And this.' He tugged her into his arms. 'I've missed you.' He kissed her softly. 'I love you, and I can't live without you.'

Her heart skipped a beat . . . two, three. 'You love me, and that's a problem?'

'It is if you don't feel the same.' His gaze searched her face. 'I want you in my life, Magee. If you don't want that, too, tell me now. Because I want forever with you, woman. I'm talking marriage. I'm talking babies, when you're ready. I'm talking — '

'Mega-commitment!'

'The whole enchilada.'

'The entire shooting gallery?'

330

'The great big greasy ball of wax.' He grinned.

Exhilaration whipped in her veins. 'But what about your expansion plans?'

'The Willoughby Bikes deal is dead. It doesn't matter. If I decide — if *we* decide — that CycleMania should open more stores, I can manage it without Nate. It might take me ten times as long to accomplish, but I can still do it. I didn't understand that when I was with Tina, because, well, she's not you. I love you, Magee. I want to be with you. Now. Not in some far-off future.'

She sighed, and he captured her mouth in a brief kiss. 'Oh, Justin, I love you, too,' she murmured. 'I've missed you so much. I love you.' His tongue traced her lips. 'And how I want you.'

He deepened the kiss. She thrust her tongue into his mouth, and a low moan rose in his throat. Hands on her upper arms, he turned them toward the desk. His hands slid down, bracing her hips as he positioned her against the desk edge. Desire swam through her, pounding, ringing. She actually heard bells.

* * *

'Damn it.' Justin tore his mouth away from Magee's. This wasn't the time for interruptions. Grabbing the cordless, he grumbled into the mouthpiece, 'Agnes, I said no calls.'

'I know, sir. I'm sorry. It's Nathan Willoughby in London. I thought he might be an exception.'

'He's not.' As Magee's fingertips caressed his jaw, Justin covered the mouthpiece and gazed at her.

'Who is it?' she whispered.

'Nate's on hold,' he whispered back. 'I swear I haven't been pushing myself on him. We haven't been in contact since they left.'

'Nate?' Magee echoed, a blush washing her face. 'Now I know how Susannah feels,' she mumbled.

'How Susannah feels about what?'

'Um . . .'

Agnes's worried voice resounded in his ear. 'I'm sorry for the misunderstanding, Mr. Kane. What should I do?'

He returned his attention to the call. 'It's okay, Agnes. Tell him I'm in a meeting. He probably wants more information about the contacts I gave him. It must be getting late over there. I'll call him back at a better time tomorr — '

The handset popped out of his grasp. 'Hey!' He looked at Magee — the little thief.

Smiling, she spoke into the phone. 'Agnes, this is Magee Sinclair. Forget what Justin said. Blame me if you have to, but please put Mr. Willoughby on.' Pressing the speakerphone button, she said to Justin, 'If I'm the reason Nate's calling, we both should hear what he has to say.'

What the hell was going on? There was only one way to find out.

Justin spoke toward the speaker. 'Please do as Miss Sinclair says,' he reassured Agnes. Then he asked Magee,

'Why would you be the reason Nate's calling?'

'Well, you see, it's like this — '

Nate's crisp English accent crackled over the speaker, interrupting her. 'Good evening. Although I guess it's good morning to you, Justin. It's not quite noon there, is it? Nathan Willoughby here.'

Magee nibbled her thumbnail. Justin slipped an arm around her waist. 'Nate, how can I help you?' he asked toward the phone. 'First, I should let you know that Magee Sinclair is with me. We have you on speaker.'

'Right,' Nate said. 'Hello to you, as well, Ti — uh, Magee. Kate's at a show with a friend, so shan't be able to chat.'

Chat? Justin looked at Magee. Why would Nate assume Magee wanted to talk to Kate?

'Um, Justin doesn't know, Nate,' Magee said toward the speaker.

'Justin doesn't know what?' Justin asked.

'That Kate and I have been talking.

Nothing to do with business,' she added quickly. 'Women stuff.'

'Yes.' Nate's voice came over the speaker. 'Magee rang Kate once or twice — '

'Three, maybe four times,' Magee added.

'Three, I believe. I'd have to ask Kate. At any rate, as you know, the girls hit it off brilliantly, and Ti — sorry, Magee wanted to ensure Kate was all right, considering things were a little sticky when we left. The upshot of all this, Justin, is that, unknown to Magee, Kate and I have rethought the whole Whistler debacle. I've spoken to my father. Despite his initial reluctance, he has conceded that the North American trade is mine to secure however I see fit. I researched my other contacts again. However, to be frank, the deal we were bashing out with CycleMania suits Willoughby Bikes best. We'd like to proceed with the final negotiations.'

Justin stared at the phone. 'You're saying you want to pursue the deal?'

Tucking in his chin, he glanced at Magee.

'I didn't have any idea,' she murmured.

'Yes, I would like to pursue the deal,' Nate responded. 'Unless you have an objection?' Hastily, he tacked on, 'Not that I wish to make a habit of what occurred in Whistler, you understand. However, given my father's rather Victorian standards, I can appreciate your situation. And, I must say, I admire your creativity.'

That was a polite way of putting it. 'Um, thank you, Nate. But — ' Justin glanced at Magee again. Moments ago, he'd told her the Willoughby Bikes deal didn't matter to him. And it truly didn't. He'd rather have her in his life than a hundred CycleMania outlets. Yet, Kate and Nate shared a great marriage *and* a successful business. Was it possible to do both?

Magee bounced in his arms. 'Say yes,' she whispered. 'Justin, what are you waiting for?' She announced toward the speaker, 'Justin says yes!'

'I do?'

She grinned, and he grinned back.

'If you say so, sweetcheeks,' he murmured. Turning to the speaker, he confirmed with Nate, 'Yes, I would be happy to resume negotiations.'

'Splendid. Kate and I adored Vancouver. We're returning the first chance we get.'

'Just say when,' Justin replied. 'Who knows, maybe your next visit can coincide with a celebration.' He ended the call with a promise to contact Kate and Nate in a few days with the arrangements for their second trip 'across the pond.' And this time CycleMania would foot the bill.

He disconnected the call.

'What's this about a celebration?' Magee asked. 'A dinner in honor of signing the deal?'

Kissing the tip of her nose, Justin snuggled her close. God, he loved this woman. 'Actually, I'm thinking of a ceremonial celebration. A wedding?' He gazed down into her upturned face. 'That is, if you'll have me. Will you marry me, Magee?'

A soft smile brightened her eyes. 'Well, I don't know. Can you live with a part-time klutz? What if I spill champagne all over myself at the wedding?'

'Then I'll lick it off you . . . in private.' Raw need burned through him. 'I love you, Magee. A few glasses of spilled wine or a dozen torn sports jackets won't change that.'

Her smile widened. 'Then, yes, Justin, I'll marry you. I'll definitely have you, too.' A sexy gleam entered her gaze. 'In fact, considering the door is locked and Agnes wouldn't dare put through another call, I believe I'll have you right now.' She kissed him. Her hands skimmed over his chest, then lower, traveling toward his belt buckle.

Justin grinned. 'In my office?'

She nodded. 'Don't worry, we can still discuss business. You know, a few marketing strategies.' She kissed him again, deeper this time. 'After all, we want to ensure full coverage . . . ' Her fingers located his belt buckle ' . . . implement a phased — ' *snick* ' — penetration . . . on a region-by-region basis.' She whisked his belt through the loops. Inhaling, she glanced at the bulge straining his pants. 'Hmm, I do believe I'm about to uncover the perfect initial region.'

'Oh baby.' Justin tugged her into his arms. 'I love it when you talk advertising.'

THE END

We do hope that you have enjoyed reading this large print book.

Did you know that all of our titles are available for purchase?

We publish a wide range of high quality large print books including:
Romances, Mysteries, Classics
General Fiction
Non Fiction and Westerns

Special interest titles available in large print are:
The Little Oxford Dictionary
Music Book, Song Book
Hymn Book, Service Book

Also available from us courtesy of Oxford University Press:
Young Readers' Dictionary
(large print edition)
Young Readers' Thesaurus
(large print edition)

For further information or a free brochure, please contact us at:
Ulverscroft Large Print Books Ltd.,
The Green, Bradgate Road, Anstey,
Leicester, LE7 7FU, England.
Tel: (00 44) **0116 236 4325**
Fax: (00 44) **0116 234 0205**

FLAMES THAT MELT

Angela Britnell

Tish Carlisle returns from Tennessee to clear out her late father's house in Cornwall — to several surprises. The first is the woman and baby she discovers living there and the second is her father's solicitor, Nico De Burgh, who was Tish's first love. Nico fights their renewed attraction because of a promise made to his foster father but Tish won't give up on him. They must share their secrets before they have any chance of a loving future together . . .

TENDER TAKEOVER

Susan Udy

To Sandy's dismay, she finds herself working for Oliver Carlton, the charismatic man who single-handedly destroyed her family — so when her hatred threatens to turn into something dangerously close to attraction, she uses all of her willpower to fight it. However, it swiftly becomes apparent that Oliver has romantic interests elsewhere, when Sandy catches sight of him with his arm around another woman . . .

HIDDEN HEARTACHE

Suzanna Ross

Doctor Emma Bradshaw's life is disrupted when Nick Rudd arrives back in town to take up a post at the GP practice where she works. It's not so easy to ignore the love of your life when you have to see him every day, but Emma is keeping her distance — Nick let her down badly in the past. Now, though, he'll do anything to rekindle the trust and love she once showed him . . .

MISTRESS OF SEABROOK

Phyllis Mallett

When her exiled father dies, Victoria comes to England from her native America to clear his name, but things go wrong from the outset. She meets her unscrupulous uncle, Landers Radbourne, and his hateful family, and begins to realise what an impossible task she has taken on. Greed and jealousy lead to a murderous climax, putting Victoria's very life in jeopardy . . .